PERFECT
HARMONY

EVA CARON

WRITERS REPUBLIC L.L.C.
515 Summit Ave. Unit R1
Union City, NJ 07087, USA

Website: *www.writersrepublic.com*
Hotline: *1-877-656-6838*
Email: *info@writersrepublic.com*

Ordering Information:
Quantity sales. Special discounts are available on quantity purchases by corporations, associations, and others. For details, contact the publisher at the address above.

Library of Congress Control Number: 2020934123
ISBN-13:   978-1-64620-265-2   [Paperback Edition]
                    978-1-64620-266-9   [Digital Edition]

Rev. date: 03/19/2020

For the boy who makes sure everyone gets on the boat

CONTENTS

This is a story about a girl I knew once. Actually, that's incorrect. I didn't really know her. No one did. There were times when it seemed like she didn't know herself.

I did, however, know her name, so I'll tell you that. Harmony. Her name was Harmony. And that's where this story begins.

———∞∞∞———

har·mo·ny
'härmənē/
noun
1. **1.**
2. the combination of simultaneously sounded musical notes to produce chords and chord progressions having a pleasing effect.

I've looked that word up a 100 times, and I still don't understand it. It's not the words I don't get, I have 20/20 vision and a twelfth grade reading level, that sentence is elementary.

I know what combination means; more than one thing mixed together. And simultaneously, that means to happen at the same time. And notes and chords, those are music terms. So basically, multiple musical sounds happening at the same time to make a new sound. That I understand.

What I don't understand is the pleasing effect part, and how it applies to me.

People say our names relate to us, that even if we don't think so at first, we all find a way to fit into them.

I know that can't be true, though, because the word harmony does not at all relate to me. The things in my body that work simultaneously, my brain and my heart, do not create a pleasing effect.

Furthermore, in no way do they form a "pleasing and consistent whole," like the second part of the definition says. If my brain and my heart worked simultaneously to make me pleasingly and consistently whole, then I wouldn't be broken.

I am, you know. Broken.

Despite all of this, it is my name.

My name is Harmony, and this is my story.

PART ONE

Mad World

I wasn't always this bad. If you looked at a picture of me from two years ago, even one, you wouldn't think I was the same person. Which gives you a sense, really, of how easy it is to break. How fragile we are.

Since this is a story about depression, and I really don't know how to begin to tell it, it seems fitting that I should start with therapy. They say write about what you know, and these past 6 months I've known little else than these 4 beige walls, the bookshelf, the FM1 radio always turned just too low, and the faint smell of cinnamon smencils.

First, let me make something clear. No kid *wants* to go to therapy. I certainly didn't. Therapy is for people who want help, who want to get better. And it works, for them, I suppose. It must, at least, because therapy is advertised, and therapists get paid, and it is, you know, a profession. But not everything works for everyone, and therapy has never worked for me. Maybe it's just that I don't deserve to get better.

But still I go. Day after day, week after week. For my mom, because I've put her through enough shit already, and it's just going to get worse. Or maybe it'll get better. Maybe after it's over, it'll get better. For them at least. I suppose I'll never know, but that can't be helped.

"You're a brave girl." she says, when she finds out how long I've kept it inside. Her name is Doctor James, and she smells like cherry coke and febreze air freshener. Nice enough, and not pushy like the others. Patient.

"You're strong, tough as nails." she's told me.

But how? I want to ask. How can I be strong if strong is living, fighting, and all I want to do is quit?

But I don't say that. I like her, so I've told her more than the others. But I still can't tell her everything.

Not about Noah.

His name was Noah, and when I first met him I had no idea how important he would become. You never really do, I suppose, because if that was how the universe worked, we would have time to prepare and it wouldn't be so surprising when you realized that someone had snuck into your heart and was innocently tearing it apart. But of course, we never have time to prepare, because of the universal principle that life sucks, and when it comes up to bite you in the ass, it rarely warns you.

That said, when I first met Noah I was 14. It was freshman year of highschool, and I didn't really know anybody, which is just about the worst way to start highschool.

I'd had friends throughout junior high, not many, but enough to invite to birthday parties and share lunch with. Hannah was the one I was closest with. Teachers called us the double h's, and though she was much prettier and more popular than I was, I trusted her with my life, and I told her everything. She was my fallback zone, my net. And then she moved away.

We still talked, of course, but talking to someone a few times a week on the phone and walking to class with them everyday are two very different things. If she had been with me my first day of Freshman year, I most likely wouldn't have ruined my life. Of course, left to my own devices, that is exactly what I did.

The first day of school, I had this awful cotton candy blue dye job in my hair, I had slammed a car door on my face the day before, and I'd woken up thirty minutes late. Needless to say, no one wanted to come up to me and start being my friend, and if they had, I probably would have killed them.

I walked into the building just as the late bell rang, miraculously found my way to homeroom on time, and collected my schedule. Exploratory Portuguese, period one, was not particularly where I wanted to be at 7:30 in the morning, but I promised my mom that this year I would try, so that's where I went.

Or rather, that's where I was *trying* to go, but the setup of Rosemont Senior High School was designed by a blind architect with dementia, I'd bet my life on it. I was wandering around, trying desperately to find some type of map, guide, or, and this is how desperate I really was, even a teacher, to point me in the right direction. What I found instead, of course, was trouble.

"Fuck." The word sprang from my lips involuntarily, as my forehead suddenly bumped against a purple, fleshy wall that stank of BO. I dropped my schedule, assigned books for English, and all of my dignity. I was tempted to just run and leave the shit behind, but without that schedule, I knew I'd spend the whole day wandering aimlessly, getting tripped over by upperclassmen.

So instead, "Sorry," I muttered, stooping to collect my shit before it was trampled by the rush of teenage traffic.

"Damn girl okay, show it off." The remark came from behind me, from the fleshy purple wall, to be more specific, and it was followed by a chorus of snickers.

I closed my eyes briefly, feeling my fists clench around my retrieved schedule, wrinkling the paper. *Keep it together, Harmony.*

I stood up to face this asshole. He was tall, too tall to be a freshman or even a sophomore for sure, but only underclassmen were supposed to be in the language wing this period, so he had to be taking remedial classes. His face was round and slightly stubbled, his chest wide. Football player, maybe. I knew I couldn't get around him and his neanderthal friends, so I tried to play it off.

"Hey if you got it, you might as well show it off, right?" I crossed my arms and raised an eyebrow, hoping he'd read the sarcasm in my tone. The truth was, I didn't "have" anything worth showing off, or at least, what I did have, I had in the wrong places.

Unfortunately, I should have known that any 17 year old stupid enough to be in Beginners Portuguese wasn't going to appreciate my humor.

"Damn okay girl, I see you." he wet his lips and put them next to my ear. "Don't worry, I like 'em feisty." His breath smelt like hot cheetos.

"I'm sure you do." I pursed my lips, and turned to leave. *Christ, just kill me already.*

That, of course, is when the smack landed on my ass. "Hold on baby girl." I could hear the smirk in his voice. I froze, but didn't turn around. That is, at least until I heard what he said next.

"Nice dye job. Tell me, does the downstairs match the upstairs?"

Sorry, mom. I lasted all of about half an hour.

Before he could catch his breath, my backpack was slung to the floor, and I was lunging for him. I'm small, but strong, and I figured I could land at least one good jab to the balls before he even knew what hit him. Fortunately and unfortunately, someone else got there first.

"Woah woah woah." the voice was unfamiliar, as was the hand that landed firmly on my chest, pushing me back. A teacher, was my first thought, or maybe a school corrections officer. But it wasn't.

"Cool off, kid." his voice was a little high for a boy his age, but somehow it still carried enough authority to curb Mr. Sexual Assault.

"Take a hike, Jason." the new kid continued. I gave Jason one last glare, my fists still clenched, chest still heaving. *No way will he listen to a kid half his size.*

But amazingly, he did.

"Whatever, man." He spit on the floor, right there in the hallway, yanked on his backpack straps, and sulked off. His friends followed him, leaving just me and the high school vigilante in the emptying hallway.

He turned to me, and I took a second to take him in. Good looking kid, I had to admit. Red and white Jordans, worn but clean, jeans that looked like they had seen better days, and what looked like a wrinkled button down that his mother had probably made him wear, which he had covered with a bulky Lakers sweatshirt. He had a strong jaw, defined eyebrows, and a high fade of thick curls. A small scar ran down his cheek. Light skin, with real dark eyes. Almost black, his eyes.

"Did he do that?" he asked, his voice so surprisingly furious that I was confused for a minute, before I realized he was talking about my black eye. I shook my head.

He let out a sigh, and in just a few seconds, his expression went from murderous to astounded. "Kid, what the hell?" he asked me, shaking his head, his eyes wide in disbelief. Amused, and maybe a little impressed. "You know he's a senior, right? You were really bouta take him right here?"

I squared my shoulders. At this point, I wasn't in the mood to be mocked anymore. "Did you see what he did? Did you hear what he said?"

He threw up his hands. "Man, I'm not saying what he did wasn't shitty. Jason's an asshole, but he's also the toughest kid in school. Everybody knows that."

"I don't." I admitted, still wary. "It's my first day."

He grinned. "I didn't think I recognized you, and I know almost everybody. Got a name?"

I sized him up, trying to find his angle. He didn't appear to be making fun of me, but he had talked to that Jason kid as though they were friends. And also, he was attractive. And I mean, really attractive. And attractive boys do not talk to girls like me, not if they can help it.

For some reason, though, I wasn't as suspicious as I normally would have been. Something about him was very calming,

"Harmony." I said finally, offering him my hand. He gave me daps, his expression thoughtful.

"Pretty." he remarked, about my name. Which was even stranger. Boys don't tell you that your name is pretty, even if they're flirting with you, and he didn't appear to be flirting. "I'm Noah."

"You sure it's not Superman?" I raised an eyebrow, but he just smiled. "Whoever you are, thanks for sparing me a suspension back there, but really, I can handle myself." I let him know. I didn't want this weird boy thinking he was being my knight in shining armour.

He laughed. "Sure seems like it. But you're new here, you said it yourself. You can't really be dumb enough to think that fighting a senior on your first day is a good idea." he raised an eyebrow, and I sighed.

"I'm not tryna be pushed around."

"You should never let yourself be pushed around." he reassured me. "But maybe it'd be better if you started off making some friends, not enemies, huh? You gotta be careful who you mess with around here. You never know what some kids might do." he was smiling as he spoke, but his eyes were serious. Warning.

I raised an eyebrow. "Should I be careful around *you*? You seem pretty comfortable around kids who put their hands on little girls."

He shrugged. "I know how to get along with people. If you know what's good for you, you'll learn how, too."

"I've never known what's good for me." I spoke without thinking, and looked at him quickly to read his reaction.

His face was unreadable, as I'd come to learn it often was. "Well, we'll have to work on that, won't we?" he smiled, and in that instant, something inside of me involuntarily crumbled. "But until then, don't worry. We're friends now. That means I got your back."

He looked at me for a second longer than seemed necessary, then he smiled, and walked away.

I was 10 minutes late to Portuguese.

After school, the rest of which had gone significantly more smoothly, I took the bus home. We lived, meaning me and my mother, in a tenement about a mile from Rosemont. It was small, all things considered, but plenty big enough for two people, plus her on again off again boyfriend, Rory. She and Rory had been "kind of" together as long as I could remember, and while I can't say I had ever seen him as a father figure, he treated my mom okay, and he went to every movie premiere with me. I guess you could say I loved the two of them the same way they loved each other- on and off.

Anyway, home, just like everything else, was fine. I had my own room, and the best part was that just outside my window was the fire escape landing, and so by putting one foot on the railing and one on my windowsill, I could hoist myself onto the roof with only minimal risk of death. Minimal, if that was how I wanted it. Too often, I imagined myself missing a step, accidentally, of course, slipping…. The house was only two stories, but standing on the roof you were 50 feet up. Sometimes I stood there, my sneakers toeing the edge, staring at the concrete. That's another thing I never told Dr. James about.

The night after my first day of high school, however, I didn't linger on my fantasies for long. Instead, swinging my legs over the edge of the shingles so they dangled like clothes hung out to dry, I pulled out my phone and called Hannah. We hadn't talked for almost a week, and while I wasn't quite sure what it was I was so anxious to tell her, I knew I wanted to tell something to someone, and I had no one else.

She picked up on the third ring, her voice harried, as always.

"Bonjour, darling! Come se va?" Hannah made it a point to master a new skill every month, "to keep me from becoming old before my time," an act that required a degree of patience I would never be able to muster. In July, it had been crocheting, and I'd received a hideous scarf that would sit useless in my closet for at least six months for my birthday in August. August had been the ukulele, and this month, September, her impossibility of choice was French.

"English, please. I'm not Joan of Arc."

"Harmony, I hear car horns. Please tell me you're not on the roof again."

"Okay, I won't tell you."

"I swear, I'll never understand what intrigues you so much about being that close to death."

"Just like I'll never understand your need to master dead languages and Pacific Island instruments."

"French is alive and well, my dear."

"Not in South Providence it isn't."

"Ah but you forget, I no longer inhabit that dreadful shithole that mascarades as a town. I'm living high and mighty here in sunny California."

"I'm not sure if Cali is known for its abundant French population either."

"Touché. But I must be prepared for my glamorous adulthood, when I shall travel overseas and meet my one true and only love in Pari. It is the city of romance, you know."

"I thought it was the city of lights."

"Quand il me prend dans ses bras, Il me parle tout bas, Je vois la vie en rose. Tell me that quote does not come from the city of love."

"I have no idea if that quote is even spoken in an actual language."

"Your ignorance is heartbreaking. I forgive you. Anywayyyy, on the topic of love, how in the world was your first day of high school? Any cute boys?"

"One grabbed my ass? Does that count?"

"I'm afraid not. You didn't notice anyone?"

"Define cute."

"OMG HARMONY! I knew it! You're coming out of your shell at last! Who is this boy?"

"What? There is no boy. I mean, there was a human person. I assume he has a penis in his possession. We exchanged pleasantries."

"Did these pleasantries involve his tongue in your mouth?"

"Hannah."

"Harmony, I'm reaching here. I can't help it that your life is as dry as a nun in a nightclub. Details child, *details*! He was cute?"

"Pretty sure. Nice eyebrows. He liked my name."

"Harmony, it sounds like you're in love. Does this future husband have a name of his own?"

"Noah?"

"Hm. Well, I shall research this mystery boy with the nice eyebrows and the wonderful taste in women. Alas, I must leave you for now, I hear the stepmonster calling. Au revoir!"

The line went dead. I sighed, staring at the screen as her contact information faded. Talking to Hannah was bittersweet; I missed her terribly, but talking to her was only a reminder of everything she was that I wasn't. It wasn't that she *had* that I didn't have, my life was no shittier than hers, maybe even better by some standards- her dad, who had practically raised me, had late stage pancreatic cancer, and their move across the country had been prompted by possible treatment options out there. Hannah would never have come right out and said it, but from what she let on, so far things had not been very successful. And yet still, she never stopped smiling. It was the way she lived. She had more personality, goals, aspirations, than I ever would. She laughed at every joke first, caught on to every math formula first. All the friends I'd had in middle school were kids *she* had met and introduced me to, in drama club, Latin class, the GSA. When we hung out with them, she was always there. She was the main attraction, and I was the backup singer. She was the superhero, and I was the sidekick. It wasn't jealousy, it was an undeniable knowledge that I was useless.

I slid my phone in my back pocket and stood up. Staring over the edge of the roof, I pictured my mangled body on the sidewalk below. I'd tip forward so the impact would snap my neck, then ricochet down my spine, breaking my pelvic and leg bones. My exterior would be relatively unscathed, once my joints were put back in order. My insides, however, would be obliterated the instant I hit the ground. It wasn't really all that different a situation than the one I was in now.

"Harmony?" I started, and almost fell at the sound of my mother's voice. Looking past the scene of my imagined corpse, I saw her standing 20 feet away from the house, next to a parked car. The light was fading fast, and the streetlights had already come on. In the sickly yellow light of the one nearest to her, she looked ten years beyond her age. Slightly smudged makeup, hair that needed a touch up dye job to hide the salt and pepper streaks that were beginning to come in near the roots. She was a little tipsy, maybe. She'd been out; I could see Rory in the car.

"I brought you takeout." She squinted, trying to read my expression. She was distracted, though, Rory was talking to her. "Honey, be careful up there. You wouldn't want to fall."

I nodded, though she couldn't see, and swung my leg over the edge, finding my footing on the railing beneath it.

"No… wouldn't want that." I muttered.

Below, Rory honked as he drove past.

"Harmony!" a hand waved in front of my face, and I snapped out of my head. "You were spacing, where do you go when you get like that?" Theresa spoke accusingly, in the exact kind of voice that would make me *not* want to tell her exactly where I went when I spaced out.

I'd known Theresa since we were 12, when Hannah met her in Intro to Poetry. We were friends… well, no. We weren't. But she and Hannah had been friends, and so we still sat together at lunch. Unlike most of the rest of our group from middle school, Theresa wasn't particularly funny or outgoing, and like me, she hadn't stuck with the main group once we moved to high school. So we sat together at lunch everyday, but that didn't mean we got along. She didn't have to tell me that she didn't like me, but she may as well have.

"I don't know. I was just thinking." I said, hoping she'd take the hint and leave me to it. She didn't, of course.

"Thinking about what? School? Classes?" her eyes narrowed as she followed my gaze across the cafeteria. "I see where you're looking, you know."

Whether I had been looking there or not, she had honed in on a group of boys standing near the vending machine. I didn't think I recognized them, I hardly recognized anyone, but I realized one kid was familiar. Or rather, his sweatshirt was. Whether I had been intentionally looking at him or not, I don't know.

"Is that Noah Andrade?" Her tone was suspicious, and I shrugged. To be fair, I didn't know his last name. "You know him?"

"We talked. Once. I wasn't looking over there." But an uneasy feeling stirred in my stomach, because I was growing more and more worried that I *had*, in fact, been looking.

Theresa shook her head disapprovingly, her thick, dark curls bouncing. "I know about him. I've heard things. Bad things. You know his brothers are drug dealers, in and out of juvie?"

I rolled my eyes, trying not to let my uneasiness show on my face. "He's not his brothers." I said evenly. Theresa drove me crazy. Always in everybody's business, when she should have just left well enough alone.

"He's related to them. And *his* record isn't the cleanest either. I see the look on your face. What did he say to you?"

I sighed. I was too tired for this shit. "He told me to be careful who I mess with."

She tossed her hair back, flipping it over her shoulders with a superior air. "If I were you, I wouldn't mess with him."

"Whatever," I muttered, and I meant it. She probably had no idea what she was talking about, and anyway, he was just a boy. A boy I had spoken to once. I looked toward the vending machine again, at the exact instant that he looked up. Our eyes met, and he smiled, just slightly. They really were black, his eyes. Endless.

I looked down. He was just a boy, and even if Theresa was wrong, the last thing I needed in my life was more trouble. This was one obstacle I could avoid easily.

Of course, as soon as you decide to stay away from someone, it becomes exactly the opposite of what you want to do.

⚬⚬⚬

High school, like everything else in my life, didn't turn out to be that bad. In theory, at least. In theory, I went to class everyday, sat at lunch everyday, went home and did my homework everyday, watched tv with my mother and sometimes Rory every night, went to bed, woke up, and repeated. And it's true that's what I did, most days. If you're thinking it doesn't sound like a half bad way to live, you're right. What you have to understand, is that my life has never been the problem. I'm sure anyone else could have lived it just fine. The problem was me.

The problem was that everyday I walked to class without remembering or caring what class I was walking to. Everyday I sat at lunch and didn't eat anything. Every night, I pulled out my homework and finished it without realizing I had started it. I ate a dinner I never tasted in front of a tv show I never watched, with two people who barely knew me. And then I lay in bed for hours, thinking about the roof.

I lived my life walking under water, where nothing could penetrate the surface. Everything I felt: anger, love, regret, existed at sea level, a level I could never quite reach. I was swimming alone in a vast ocean, and the sun only warmed the first foot of water. Below that, I was so numb I didn't even know I was freezing.

This was something I *had* told Dr. James, one day in her colorless office with its stock photo images still in the picture frames on the wall. I picked at a seam on my jeans and told her about a study I read on kids with Congenital Insensitivity to Pain and Anhydrosis, or CIPA disorder. These kids could suffer bruises, lacerations, even broken bones, and have no idea. They just didn't feel it.

"Do you think you may have CIPA?" she'd asked, scribbling on her notepad. She never put it down, that notepad, but I didn't mind. I would have been more nervous if she'd spent the whole session staring at me, and

I think she knew that. Also, it interested me that on some days I would talk nonstop for the whole hour, and she would only take down three sentences of observations. On other days, when I just sat and stared at the wall for the entire time, she'd have over a page of notes.

"No, I don't have it the way that those kids do." I closed my eyes, and saw myself treading water in the middle of the ocean. I saw my mangled body on the sidewalk outside my house.

Her pencil stopped moving.

"It's like I have it in my mind. I have congenital insensitivity to pain in my *mind*."

"Hey!" Noah shouted in my ear at the same instant he grabbed my sides.

I jumped, spinning around to glare at him, only to be met with a laugh. I tried to keep from smiling, but one look at his face and it was impossible.

"Hey, Superman. Can I help you?" I raised an eyebrow. Everything this kid did was unexpected.

"Do you have gym after lunch? I'm walking with you." He grinned, and slid into the empty chair next to me. He leaned across the table and opened my bag of fritos, helping himself to a few.

"What if I'm not going to gym?" I was trying to ignore Theresa, Noah certainly was. Out of the corner of my eye, I could see her staring at me from across the table.

"I know you are. So am I, so we might as well go together, right?" He followed my gaze across the table to Theresa and, seeming to read my expression, shifted his chair, effectively blocking me from her view.

"Are you a freshman?" I was curious. He looked young, an underclassman for sure. But I'd seen him in the halls with kids from every grade, always looking completely comfortable. And I hadn't forgotten the tone of authority in his voice the day he had called Jason off. Even I knew it wasn't likely for a senior to let himself be bossed around by a freshman.

"Yeah. I went to Massasoit Middle. You?" He reached out, seemingly subconsciously, and tucked my hair behind my left ear.

I raised an eyebrow. "Harrington."

"Why are you laughing at me?"

"You're very comfortable around other people, aren't you?" I wanted to feel uncomfortable, here this boy who I barely knew was sitting with me for no reason, sharing my bag of chips without asking, and playing with my hair. For some reason though, I didn't mind.

He shrugged, leaning back to give daps to a couple of boys who walked by. If he noticed the weird looks they gave us, he didn't say anything. "I like people. You don't, do you?"

I was startled. Not because he had read my mind or anything, I *did* like people. It was myself that I didn't like, but it saddened me a bit to know that maybe it came off as me not liking anyone else. "I never said that."

He looked at me for a moment, his dark eyes locked on mine as though he would have been perfectly comfortable to sit there and stare at me for the rest of the day. *Christ, he's weird*, was my thought, and for the first time, I felt slightly uneasy. I looked down.

"So," he recovered quickly, and picked up my assigned English book from where it lay on the table. "What's it about?"

It was The Handmaid's Tale, and although he flipped through it, I could tell he was more interested in the notes I'd left in the margins than the book itself.

"Sex and politics."

"Sex and politics." he repeated, and I could hear the smile in his voice. "What would you know about that, huh?"

I finally turned back to him, ready to defend myself if he was trying to make fun of me. If he was asking what I thought he was asking, then he definitely already knew the answer. One look at me, and anyone would know the answer. But his expression wasn't mocking, or even curious. Amused, maybe. He knew, for sure he knew, but he wanted to see how I would play it off.

"Whatever's written in the book." I said finally, and his eyes brightened. I felt a feeling of acceptance, as though he had approved of the response I'd given.

I wanted to ask him what *he* might know about it, but I shook off the urge. A boy who looked like that... he had to know quite a bit. Luckily, the arrival of a girl about my age with long acrylic nails saved me.

Sweeping her hair over her shoulder, she leaned over and whispered into Noah's ear. His eyes widened, and he turned to her with a grin. "Oh shit, for real?"

"Yea, you should see it." Her smile was friendly, but her body language betrayed alternative intentions. The way she played with her hair as she spoke to him, how she still hadn't moved her hand from his shoulder. Not that I was paying attention.

He stood up, and touched my arm as he left. "Rain check. I'll catch you later, Million Dollar Baby." To the girls' credit, she smiled at me before they left.

I didn't watch them walk away, I didn't need to. I could, however, see Theresa starting to open her mouth, so I got up and left too. I had no reason to stay, *not now that he's gone,* it occured to me suddenly. I straightened my mouth, not sure what emotion I was struggling to keep off my face. And honestly, if you're thinking it was jealousy that I felt, you wouldn't even be entirely right. Noah didn't owe me anything, not his friendship, or any kind of attention otherwise. The fact that he chose to give it to me anyway, if only briefly, should have been nothing but appreciated. And I *did* appreciate it, don't get me wrong. But there was something too peculiar about it to be ignored. He was popular, he was personable, he was cute. And me, I just wasn't. I wasn't anything much in general, at least not anything good. If he was getting mysterious, hiding-something-beneath-the-surface vibes from me, he couldn't have been more wrong. The only things I had beneath the surface were things that nobody would have wanted to find. He made me feel special, but I knew that I wasn't, and every moment that I was with him I was sure that the next he would look at me and realize it.

Nevertheless, I found myself fingering a piece of my hair, wondering how long it would be before his fingerprints rubbed off of it.

My life, unfortunately, went on even when Noah wasn't a central player in it. He came and went, just like everyone else, when it was convenient for him. In some ways, it was the only thing he had in common with *anyone* else.

Over the next few months, he showed up unexpectedly, and every time he did, it was as if he didn't remember that it had been days or even weeks since we'd spoken. He went out of his way to call to me from across the cafeteria, came out of nowhere to pull my hair or grab my sides, even walked me to class.

Everything he did had a physicality to it, it was as though he never stopped moving. He hugged everyone, as though it were the way people greet each other on a regular basis. It only took a week or so for it to become his standard greeting for me. Sometimes he just came up behind me and wrapped his arms around me for a minute, then left without a word. It was strange at first, not because I had anything against physical contact, I just wasn't used to it. But I found I came to look forward to the days when he would run up to me and squeeze me so hard I was lifted off my feet.

Then, of course, were the days when it was like I didn't exist at all. He was the friendliest person I'd ever met, but he was also the least consistent. He hung out with everybody, jocks, stoners, band kids, nerds, and I admired that. He wasn't worried about being judged by anybody, whereas I was constantly worried about being judged by *everyone*. Of course, some kids didn't appreciate the things I found so intriguing, the teachers certainly didn't, but most people were very taken with him, I could tell. Especially the girls. They followed him everywhere, but whether he was actually with one of them I could never tell. In some ways, he treated every girl as though he wanted them, myself included. He could make you feel like the -only person on earth with just one conversation, but as soon as he left, and he always did, reality came crashing back in harder than ever before.

I tried to spot a pattern in his comings and goings, but as far as I could tell, he just bounced around from person to person on a routine only he could control. He was more unpredictable than my menopausal mother, and while in a way it made me like him more, in another, I felt somewhat used. Every time it seemed like we started to get somewhere, he'd disappear for a week. Sometimes, the disappearance was literal, and he'd return to school after a few days with a black eye or a busted lip, and everybody knew to stay clear. Whatever happened to him, he never wanted to talk about with anyone, which I was quick to learn.

It happened on a Monday in October, the first time he came back to school with a broken face. He hadn't been there since Wednesday, and while it in no way really affected me, I found myself looking for him every morning, hoping that I'd see a faded Lakers sweatshirt walking down the hall.

It wasn't until Monday, however, that I did. First period, I lingered outside my class, Victorian Literature, scanning the halls. I was about to turn in when I saw him. It was as if he had never left, he bounced down the hallway like he always did, pulling on one guys backpack and giving a side hug to another as he passed. His eyes were as bright as always, but when he turned I saw a long shadow under one, and a darkening that closed his eyelid partway. No one else said anything, so I certainly didn't, and instead went to class. I had almost forgotten about it by Chemistry.

"Did you hear about Noah this morning?" the voice came from behind me, and I paused while copying the equation off the board. It was third period, and I had nearly convinced myself that what I'd seen had been a trick of the light.

I turned my head to the side slightly, so my peripheral vision could catch who'd spoken. It was the same girl who had pulled him away at lunch that day in September, the one with the long acrylics and shiny black hair. She was talking to her friend, but made no point to keep her voice down.

"Mr. McCane asked him if he got the black eye in a fight. When Noah didn't answer," she paused, and her voice lowered, "McCane told him he bet he had, and that he was just like his father."

"No." the other girl sounded shocked. "He said that? What'd Noah do?"

"Gio told me he threw a chair, and walked out."

I couldn't help it, I turned around. "He threw a chair?" One of the girls looked at me as though I had no right to ask, but half the class could have heard them. The girl with the acrylics, however, gave me a once over, then nodded slightly. I was reminded of the way Noah had seemingly sized me up the day I'd met him.

"Yea. He's got a really quick temper." She smiled, and nudged her friend, who was still glaring at me. She rolled her eyes and turned away to dig around for something in her backpack. Her friend ignored her, and turned back to me, tapping her nails on the table between us. "You guys are friends, right?"

I shrugged. "I guess. He always seemed pretty chill to me."

The other girl sat up again, having produced a pocket juul from her bag. She checked to make sure the teacher was occupied, then took a hit, offering it to the girl beside her.

"He is… usually. Certain things, well, certain things set everybody off, right?" she smiled, accepting the vape and then offering it to me. I shook my head. Smoking had never been my thing. I realized I was tracing my finger across the veins on the inside of my wrist, and quickly moved my arm off the table. I looked up at her defiantly. *Sure, go ahead, ask what sets me off.* But she didn't.

Instead, she introduced herself as Alana, and her friend as Lexi. We talked for the rest of the class, and they passed the juul between them until the bell rang. While I didn't feel like any of the questions I had about Noah had been answered, (they'd changed the subject quickly), they were nice enough, even Lexi.

The rest of the year passed similarly. I held my ground around the kids in all my classes, and while I can't say I made any actual friends, by December I wasn't eating lunch with Theresa anymore, so that was something at least. Alana and Lexi let me hang around with their friends every now and then, an assortment of white girls who thought it was okay to say the n-word, with iphones as big as their faces and matching sweat suits that said PINK across the ass. Their topics of conversation had little range beyond who was sleeping with who and what boys were going to fight after school, but they weren't really so bad. If I was quiet enough, it was as if they forgot I was there, spare the occasional question about where I'd bought my jacket or what kind of mascara I used.

Noah came around there group often enough, usually with an acknowledgment of "females," to which they would all roll their eyes and groan, only to giggle incessantly as soon as he was gone. They were all "going" with some of his friends, Giovani and Justin and Jaideson, but it was no secret who it was they were really interested in. He must have noticed, and he must have been sleeping with at least a few of them, but for some reason, none of them ever had him for good.

I watched all of this happen as an audience member observing a sitcom about high school. As I did in everything else, I existed in their group as filler, a piece of the wall that happend to breathe, existing but never mattering. If I had a bad day they never noticed, neither did anyone else in any of the friend circles I slipped in and out of. I didn't resent them for it, if I had asked them for help then who knows, maybe they would have been helpful. The fact that I never asked was on me, not anyone else.

I knew I was falling into the same pattern that had been detrimental to me in middle school, and I knew that I was doing the opposite of what I'd promised my mother, and I know now exactly what Doctor James would have said about it- keeping everything inside was a foolproof way to explode. I knew all of this, and I let it happen anyway. I'm not sure if a part of me hungered for my own destruction, or if I just saw it as inevitable. Either way, I was self destructing, and no one noticed.

I said I'd tell you about what led me to where I am now, and I said that even 6 months ago it wasn't nearly this bad. That's both true, and a gross understatement. 6 months ago, near the end of my sophomore year, my mother decided that there was something seriously wrong with me, and that if I didn't get real help soon, I'd be a lost cause. What she didn't know was that there had been something seriously wrong for a long time, and I had always been a lost cause.

I want to say that it started in middle school, but even that wouldn't be totally accurate. I became aware of it in middle school, and other people started to become aware a few years later, but it had really begun long before that.

I think I was around six years old when it occurred to me for the first time that someone else could have lived my life better than I did.

For my sixth birthday, I got an American Girl Doll for Christmas. It was Kit, and she was the first real love of my life. I played with her for years, probably a few too many, and I read every book and mystery story about her cover to cover. When the Kit movie came out, Rory and I went to see it opening day. I was so intrigued by all the adventures she went on and the mysteries she solved, I remember asking Rory on the way home from the movies, "Why can't my life be as exciting as Kit's?" He laughed, and told me that life always seems more exciting when you're looking at someone else's. I sat on that for awhile, and pondered it in my own little kid way. What was the point of reading fantastic and interesting stories if all they were going to do was make my own life seem duller? For awhile, I tried to live the way that Kit and all the other girls I read about growing up lived. There were no mysteries to solve in the suburbs, so naturally I'd decided that the only reasonable thing to do was run away.

I didn't know where I was going, only that I planned to go alone, and that I didn't plan to come back. I remember packing my backpack with the essentials, (underwear, Hershey's bar, all my Kit books) and planning out my trip. Maybe I would end up homeless, or hungry, or lonely. Maybe I would even die. The idea was so foreignly thrilling that I reveled in it.

But obviously, not everything went according to plan. I hadn't made it five miles before the police picked me up. I was genuinely surprised by my mother's hysterical reaction when she asked me why on earth I had wanted to run away and I calmly told her I didn't want to live my life. *Who would want to live it?* was my thought at the time.

I soon found out, however, that the answer was "a lot of people." As the years passed and I went to school and made friends, I learned that other kids were perfectly content with their lives. Simple things made them so happy- a trip to the movies, snack time at school, birthday presents. Those things made me smile too, of course, but an emptiness had settled in my core that nothing could seem to fill. Even my Kit books no longer lit up my world. I felt betrayed by Kit. She had taught me that I could live an exciting life just relishing in the everyday goings on around me, but that lesson had been a lie. Other kids could do it, but I could not. By the time I was 10, I had figured out the truth. Stories like Kit's and Anne of Green Gables' and Nancy Drew's and all the rest were written to *inspire* little girls, and they did. They just didn't work on me.

I carried the weight of knowing that I would never be satisfied with my life with me into middle school, where it morphed and developed and took on different forms, but never really went away. I met kids with lives much worse than mine, like Hannah, who still managed to find the good in them. Whereas they were happy, I was miserable, and I felt terribly guilty about it. Who was I to dare to complain about my life just because it was a little boring, when others never complained, and their lives were total shit? I disgusted myself. I couldn't understand why I could never just suck it up and deal, and I grew to hate myself for it. By seventh grade, I had begun to think it would be better if I didn't exist at all.

I sat on my bed every day and tried to force some type of meaning into myself. But it's impossible to find something when you don't know what you're looking for, and the harder I tried, the farther I slipped away. The farther everything slipped.

There are days and even weeks of my life that I don't remember, when everything was a blur of going through the motions and smiling and nodding and waking up somewhere without remembering ever having fallen asleep. My mother, to her credit, despite probably thinking I was insane, took notice, and then appropriate action by immediately moving me off her plate. She didn't know how to help me, and while I don't blame her for not trying harder to figure it out, she probably could have. Instead, the solution was to shuffle me off to a variety of different therapists, whom I dutifully smiled and lied to, because I knew what they didn't. No one was going to save me, because I wasn't worth saving. There's nothing more pathetic than killing yourself from the inside out, and I knew that any person who willingly did that was a pretty useless addition to the human race. I hated myself for hating myself, and nothing was going to change that.

I honestly don't know how I managed to survive as long as I did. Actually, that's not entirely correct. I do know how. There were two people who got me through the first fourteen years of my life, and no, they were not my mother and Rory. I don't want to discredit the impact that they did have, because it wasn't insignificant. However, there is something less memorable about the love that you receive from people who are supposed to love you. The fact that my mother loved me wasn't extraordinary, and I know that many kids aren't even fortunate enough to have their mother's love, but that falls into the category of unusual. My mother loved me, yes, but she was my mother, she had to love me. And Rory loved me, I know he did, but he loved my mom, and so by association he was obligated to put up with me too.

No, the two people who came into my life in its early stages and loved me for God knows what reason were my best friend, Hannah, and her father.

From the ages of six to 14, I spent every minute of free time I had at the Santanuno's. Hannah and I were closer than best friends, we were like sisters, and her dad… well, suffice to say that it took me around three years to figure out that he wasn't actually my dad, too. Mr. Santanuno was the type of guy who actually hung out with us when we had sleepovers, instead of just sending us upstairs to keep ourselves entertained. He brought us both to work with him at the construction site on "bring your kids to work day." He showed us the movie station where classic movies were edited so swears and sex scenes were cut out, so that we could have the cultural experience without being scarred for life. He let us try lipstick samples and perfume dabs on him, and he pretended not to notice when we were eating cookie dough straight out of the freezer. I know that kids aren't supposed to be friends with their parents, but with a guy like Mr. Santanuno as your dad, you couldn't really help it.

Except that he wasn't my dad. And Hannah wasn't my sister. And when they moved to California, I didn't go with them.

I stayed in Rhode Island, and with them gone, I continued to spiral into myself.

Flash forward to six months ago, when my mother finally snapped. She's never yelled at me like that before or since, so much and so unrelentingly that I stumbled and actually passed out from her tirade. Enough was enough, for her at least, after my latest therapist suggested a brief stint in hospital would be beneficial to me. Either that, or immediate disposal of every sharp object in the house, scissors, knives, she even recommended confiscating nail files.

My mom wasn't having any of it. "You will pull yourself together and get better, do you fucking hear me? You're not stupid, you're not crazy, I don't know what the fuck is wrong with you Harmony but god help me you will figure it out. Here, in this house, not in any goddamn hospital. You are FINE. Pull your head out of your ass and realize that you are *fine*. I grew up with jack shit, Harmony, and I managed. I did it. So you bet your ass you should be able to, too." Rory, who had given up on trying to calm down my mother at this point, had nodded for me to leave the room. As I did, something struck the wall where my head had just been. The kitchen scissors, thrown across the room. "Do you wanna take these with you, Harmony?!" my mother screamed hysterically. She was broken, and I had broke her, but no matter how hard I tried, I couldn't cry. Instead, I climbed onto the roof.

The next morning, Rory drove me to school. I hadn't heard them arguing the night before- usually when she was mad at me, it transpired into an argument with him. Instead, the eerie quiet that had filled the house had made me wonder if they were still breathing.

He was quiet on the ride to the school, and when he picked me up, we didn't drive home. He took me across the bridge to the nice part of town, and pulled up in front of an aesthetically pleasing brick building. I didn't ask questions when he told me the room number, I knew what was going on. As I got out of the car, he opened his mouth, as if wanting to say something. Then he closed it.

The office was down a hall, past 12 doors, the last one on the left. *Dr. Patricia James,* was written on the door. I opened it, and she looked at me, an average sized 15 year old girl with dark shadows under her ordinary brown eyes, and I looked at her, a slightly above average sized 40 something year old woman with skin darker than mine but eyes that were lighter. Warmer. More open.

Then, raising an eyebrow, she said, "You look like shit."

I liked her immediately, and she liked me. She thought I was hilarious, and when I told her that I was really just a bitch, and people tended to think I was joking, she laughed for a solid 5 minutes. I've seen her once a week for the past six months, she's the only therapist who's lasted more than two. I figured out pretty early on that I couldn't lie to her, not like i had lied to everyone else, because Dr. James said she could smell bullshit a mile away, and she hated people who tried to make her swallow it. So I told her the truth, enough of it to keep her satisfied, at least.

I remember the day I told her about CIPA. it was right after she told me I was "tough as nails," and I'd replied that no, I wasn't tough, I was indifferent. I explained about the kids who couldn't feel pain, and I told her that I felt nothing emotionally. I was swimming in freezing water.

She looked up from her pad, and her pencil stopped moving. She locked eyes with me, something she rarely did.

"Nothing makes you feel? Nothing at all?"

PART TWO

Say

"Noah." I said reluctantly, making eye contact with him.

He stood up from his spot on the bleachers and joined my team, grinning. He was a kid who could always count on being picked for a team in gym class, unlike me, who could only ever count on being picked by him.

I usually kept a low profile in *all* my classes, gym most of all, for obvious reasons. But I couldn't escape being chosen as a team captain eventually, much to my dismay.

Noah grabbed a purple pinney, the height of high school fashion, and fell dramatically onto the floor behind me, before straightening up to lean uncomfortably close over my shoulder. Besides gym, we had Portuguese together, and on the days when he was in a good mood, he usually walked with me. Today had been one of those days, when we walked across the school while he told me everything that was on his mind and then spent the remaining time trying to figure out what was on mine. I didn't mind, his mindless stream of endless chatter was always interesting, and while I'm sure he was not partial to who his audience was, I was always flattered when it happened to be me. When we were together, it felt like time stopped, and we existed in a world where the differences between us fell away. He made it feel like nothing mattered outside of the moment.

23

In class, however, it was a different story. Being popular and athletic, Noah's time to shine was gym class, where he became a 12 year old boy again- racing to get the best basketball, hogging the soccer ball down the field, showing off when he scored. My low profile did not coincide with his bodacious one, but to his credit, everytime he was assigned as a team captain, I was always his first pick, so it only seemed fair that he should be mine.

"Pick one more boy, Harmony." Mr. Waiter said. Before I could even open my mouth, an all too familiar voice whispered in my ear.

"Andy. Or Devante." I turned slowly, raising an eyebrow at Noah. I could feel the eyes of the entire class on me, but as soon as I looked at him, I forgot they were even there. This was just Noah, and he was being annoying as hell.

"Excuse me, who died and made you captain?" I could hear laughter from the kids around me, and even Mr. Waiter and the other teachers. But my eyes were on him.

"You're lucky I picked you at all after the way you were playing yesterday." I went on. He raised his eyebrows, and his mouth hung open a bit, but his eyes were as bright as always. "Shut up and let me finish?"

He leaned back, wet his lips and smirked slightly, amused and maybe a little impressed. "Sure Harmony. My bad."

I rolled my eyes and turned back around. "Drew." I said calmly, but my heart was beating a hundred miles a minute.

My eyes drifted to Noah throughout the entire game, as he scored 2 goals and held up the entire second half after accidentally tripping a girl, just to triple check that she was okay. We didn't talk again, however, until Mr. Waiter called for the teams to switch, and we went back to the bleachers.

I sat alone, as per usual, maybe 5 feet away from the rest of the team. It wasn't more than a couple minutes, however, until someone bounced up beside me.

"*Hey.*" He said loudly, jumping up the benches two at a time before plopping down next to me. He bumped his shoulder against mine, leaning in at what should have been an uncomfortably close distance. My body tensed and relaxed at the same as I inhaled muted scents of pot, Old Spice, sweat, ranch, and boy. Mostly, though, he just smelled clean, like no matter what he did, (or smoked), no smell could overpower the feeling that his clothes were fresh out of the dryer. He was wearing a purple Lakers t shirt and Adidas sweatpants that were not *un*flattering. I looked up to see him smirking at me, and quickly averted my eyes.

"I think you might be the only Lakers fan in the whole school." I said by way of greeting.

He shrugged, glancing at his t shirt as though he'd forgotten he was wearing it. "My dad's a Lakers fan, so I guess I always have been. Bulls aren't bad either though." He nodded toward my faded hoodie.

"It's my dads." I explained, which was true, but wasn't why I was wearing it. I hadn't seen my father since I was two- I was a Bulls fan because Hannah's older brother also happened to be one, and when we were little he took us to a game once.

"Have you ever seen a game with him? Your dad, I mean." Noah asked. I shook my head. "We don't- he's not…. No. I haven't. Have you?" He smiled, and his eyes warmed. "No. 'he's not' either."

I nodded, and we sat in understanding silence for awhile. He was watching the game, so I figured it was safe for me to look at him. He really was just one of those people you could never get tired of looking at- I could tell what was happening in the game just by watching his eyes follow it.

When I reached out to fix his shirt collar, I did it without thinking. He didn't start, which made me think he hadn't been as oblivious of me as I had assumed. Instead he glanced down, and gently grabbed my wrist.

I wore long sleeves just about every day, and on the days when I didn't, I woke up early to apply concealer to my arms from wrist to elbow. It was last period, however, and the makeup had rubbed off. When my sweatshirt sleeve was pushed up, as it was now, there was nowhere to hide.

He turned my hand over, and ran his thumb lightly against the inside of my wrist. I wanted to pull my arm away but didn't see the point, for several reasons. One, he definitely already knew. We'd had gym together for almost five months, and often I rolled my sleeves up. There's no way he hadn't already seen. Two, and more importantly, I knew it couldn't be a turn off, because for something to turn off it had to have once been turned on.

Still, I felt on edge with his eyes staring at the years of scars that overlapped each other. Other people's opinions on what I did to myself didn't matter, but for some reason his did. I didn't want to be ugly in front of him, even if he hadn't ever seen me as the opposite. The cuts... they were so blatant, so unavoidable, and his thumb was touching them. I felt naked, I felt gross, I felt pathetic. God, I hated myself.

"Why do you do it?" His question was curious but not sympathetic or prying, and as usual, his expression was impossible to read. He didn't look at me, his eyes didn't leave my ruined skin.

I shrugged, and reminded myself to breathe. "I don't know if you'd get it." Which was true. As little as I understand him now, over a year later, I understood him even less then.

He smiled slightly, finally releasing my wrist and leaning back against the wall. "Try me."

I looked at him, rubbing my arm self consciously. "To feel? I guess. Like, do you ever just, not feel anything?"

He didn't answer, but instead asked, "Do you feel anything right now?" He was leaning back, almost casually, but there was nothing casual about the way he was looking at me.

I swallowed. "Right now, yes. Usually, no." He waited. "Usually, it's like I feel everything with the volume turned down low, and I can never turn it high enough to really hear it." I wanted him to understand, but I was afraid that he wouldn't care.

"Does it hurt?"

"Yeah." I nodded, looking at his shoulder. Looking at his eyes was too hard. "It hurts." My voice was barely a whisper.

"Does it help?" He had lowered his voice too.

I closed my eyes. I saw blood staining the water in my sink pink as I washed my arms. I saw the toes of my sneakers edging over my roof. "No." I opened my eyes. "It doesn't."

"So why?"

"Because as soon as I start thinking about it, I can't not do it. And as soon as I start doing it, I can't stop. It's like- it's like I'm addicted to it. Kind of." It was the only way I could think to describe it, but maybe it was the only way he'd even kind of understand.

He was quiet- he was watching the game- and I was beginning to think we were done with the conversation when he suddenly said, "Sometimes, I look at myself and I feel like I see only what everybody else sees, and

that's all I've seen for so long that I've forgotten what I really look like."
He turned to me. "Is it like that?"

I shrugged. "I don't know. Maybe. But please don't cut yourself."

I heard him laugh and turned back to him. "There are other ways to feel you know, Harmony."

He was smiling, but his eyes were serious. I had that feeling again, like he could have been content to look at me for the rest of the day. And I was sure, suddenly, that if he did, if he even kept staring at me for just another five seconds, there'd be something more than air between us. There'd be something *more*.

I looked away.

Freshman year finished uneventfully.

I went to school everyday, and bounced amongst a variety of different therapists, smiling and lying dutifully. My mother asked me periodically how I was feeling, and the answer never changed. "I'm fine, mom."

And I was, for the most part. I was beginning to think that maybe if I could just manage to live with myself for the next few years, my mind would sort itself out eventually. I wasn't getting better, no, but I hadn't been getting worse. I did, for awhile, convince myself that I was fine, that I would be fine. To tell you that I couldn't have been more wrong would just be me getting ahead of myself, so I won't tell you that.

Instead, I'll tell about how Hannah came to visit in February, and how her dad and stepmom took us to New Hampshire to ski for a weekend, and how we got drunk on wine coolers and she told me she'd "finally given it up" to a boy in her calculus class ("But I don't think it will last, darling. He's such a *boy*, and a woman like me needs a man.") I told her I had made a couple real friends, which was true. A few of the kids in my classes thought I was funny, and had adopted me into their group of quirky band kids and student council members. I still hung out with Alana and her vape obsessed friends every so often, to the horror of the band kids. I'd realize later that, like a certain someone I knew, I found it pretty easy to get along with different kinds of people.

In April, I finally abandoned the blue dye job, and spent an hour with my mother redying my hair, (and hands), a deep purplish red. She said I looked like a real teenager, and Rory said it made me look like Ozzy Osbourne. Alana said it was hot, Hannah said it was very sophisticated (and "about time"), Theresa said she couldn't understand what was so wrong with my natural hair color, and my new friends gave me a variety of opinions ranging from "cool" to "in style." Noah, who continued to pop in and out of my life on his own accord, told me I looked like a mermaid.

All in all, you'd think I was feeling pretty good about high school, and I was, on good days. I found jokes genuinely funny, I grew to deeply care for my friends, teachers found me witty and mature, and my English teacher even told me she thought I had a real shot in a career as a writer. I should have been happy. I *was* happy.

I had a little over a year to live.

I should have suspected that things were going to turn to shit after the way Sophomore year started. I should have realized that if I could never trust anyone else, I'd definitely never be able to trust myself.

That being said, I don't blame Noah for what happened. I didn't then, and I don't now. The things that he did and said that year shouldn't have surprised me, and the fact that they did is no one's fault but mine. I was more than halfway in love with him by the time I turned 15, and that was entirely my mistake.

We only saw each other once that summer, and that one meeting was enough to make me dread seeing him ever again. We didn't plan to run into each other, it was an unfortunate occurrence that was, as usual, entirely my doing. I shouldn't have been there, but I was, because I always managed to be exactly where I shouldn't.

It was August, I had just turned 15. Rory, my mom and I went to see a drive in one night double feature of Dirty Dancing and The Breakfast Club, two movies which summed up a decade perfectly. Hannah sent me an embroidered likeness of Hello Kitty that she had made herself, and we skyped for an hour. Not a bad way to spend a 15th birthday, over all, and I was in a good mood when I went out for a walk the next day, a Saturday.

Usually, a few boys hung around shooting hoops by the middle school on Saturday afternoons, and I liked to sit in the shade and read while I watched them. On that particular Saturday, however, I arrived at the school to find that it was more crowded than usual.

Six kids my age were spread out under my usual tree, and the smell and smoke coming from their direction made me immediately change course. If I went home smelling like pot, my mother would have it in for me for sure.

"Harmony!" I had just turned away when I heard my name. One of the girls had broken away from the group, and I recognized her shiny dark hair immediately, though it was considerably shorter than the last time I'd seen it.

"Hey, Alana." I returned her hug. "Cute haircut."

"You like it?" She ran her fingers through her bobbed hair before walking back to the group. I knew her well enough to know she expected me to follow her, so I did, reluctantly.

I recognized most of the kids under the tree, Lexi and Gio and Devante. There was only one girl who was unfamiliar, she was white with thick curls and acne, which she was trying to hide with too much makeup. I wouldn't have noticed her at all, really, if she hadn't been sitting in Noah Andrade's lap.

"Hey, guys." I tried to keep my voice even. Lexi, who had never entirely warmed to me, smiled, and the two boys gave me daps.

"You look good, Harmony." Devante smiled at me.

Alana nodded toward the third girl. "That's Gianna."

Gianna didn't smile, but instead brought her blunt to her lips and deliberately blew smoke in my face. I didn't cough, and I didn't smile at her either.

I looked at Noah, but he seemed to be intent on pretending I didn't exist. His mouth was a thin line, and he refused to even glance in my direction. For some reason, the smoke, maybe, my eyes began to sting.

"So how's your summer, Harm?" Alana fell onto the grass beside Lexi and started rolling paper she had produced from nowhere.

"It's ok. I turned 15 yesterday." I shifted from foot to foot, trying to be unaware of Gianna's eyes on me, and Noah's lack thereof.

"Girllll, happy birthday." Alana squealed. "You shoulda told me. Do anything fun?"

I shrugged. I liked Alana and Gio, I really did, but it wouldn't have taken a genius to figure out that this wasn't my scene. The atmosphere was off, we could get away with hanging out in school, but we would never really be friends outside of it. Alana was reaching to work me into conversation, and while I could tell her intentions were good, she should have just let me leave.

Lexi finished rolling her joint and lit up, passing it first to Devante and then to Alana, who had the courtesy to blow her mouthful of smoke at the sky, not my face.

She held the blunt out to me, but I shook my head. My clothes smelling like pot was one thing, my breath smelling like it was another.

"You don't smoke?" I looked up. Gianna was looking at me accusingly. She took another drag while her left hand crept up Noah's shoulder to the back of his neck. He visibly tensed, but still said nothing.

"It's bad for your skin. But I guess you already know that." I said coolly, looking at her pointedly.

Lexi coughed into her hand and Gio snickered under his breath. Gianna raised an eyebrow, and her superiorly teasing facade dropped.

"Was that supposed to be funny?" Her voice was ice.

"I mean, don't tell me I'm wrong." My eyes were on her hazel green ones. She had been testing me, and she thought she was going to get the better of me for sure. But I had the upper hand now, everybody knew it.

"Look, if you're not gonna smoke, then leave." Noah spoke for the first time. His voice was like I'd heard it only once before- when he asked me if Jason had given me my black eye. Furious.

"Noah." Alana said, shocked. Out of the corner of my eye, I could see her staring at him.

He turned to me finally. His dark eyes, usually so warm and welcoming, were cold, hard, and red around the edges. "I mean it. Get lost."

I looked at the ground. The smoke was getting thicker, and my eyes stung horribly. *Leave, Harmony.* But I couldn't. I couldn't move, until he did.

He stood up, pushing Gianna off his lap. In two steps he was less than three feet from my face, and he threw the smoldering end of his blunt at my feet. No one said anything, not Gianna, either of the boys, or even Alana. I remembered what she had told me about Noah on the first day we talked. *Certain things, well, certain things set everybody off, right?*

I forced myself to look at him. He held my gaze for only a second, and I don't know who's eyes were blurry, his or mine, but I could barely see him. "Fuck off, Harmony. Now."

And I did. It took everything I had not to run, but instead I walked away slowly, forcefully.

I wanted to feel angry, I wanted to feel heartbroken or embarrassed or betrayed. But instead I felt nothing. I could hardly feel myself breathing.

I got home without realizing I had been walking in that direction. I let myself in through the backdoor, so I wouldn't have to walk by my mother in the living room. Stands With a Fist, Rory's cat, who lived at our house because his apartment didn't allow animals, meowed indignantly at my feet. I opened the fridge and found the cat food, then dropped an unattractive lump in his bowl. "Fed the cat, mom." My voice didn't sound like mine. It didn't sound like anything.

Rory's keys were on the counter. Along with the key for his apartment, our house, the garage where he worked, and his busted Kia, he had one of those multi use utility tools on his key chain. The kind with a corkscrew, a bottle opener, a nail file. And a pocket knife.

I walked past the counter and up the stairs to my room, but it wasn't until I'd shut the door behind me that I realized the keys were in my hand. How they got there, I didn't know. I didn't remember picking them up. I hadn't remembered rolling up my sleeve either, but suddenly I found myself staring at my bare wrist. Six months before, Noah's thumb had been tracing my skin. Now the blade of the knife was.

Why do you do it?

I heard his voice, and ran the blade against my wrist. It stung, but didn't break the skin.

To feel, I guess.

I tried to feel something, anything, but nothing came. I heard Gianna's voice. *Was that supposed to be funny?* I heard Noah's. *Fuck off, Harmony.* I tried to turn the volume up, but it was like I was hearing them from underwater. I was numb, my body was stiff and cold.

Then I felt a stinging in my wrist again. I looked down. This time, a thin line of blood ran down my arm.

Does it help?

No, it didn't, but I couldn't stop. I was transfixed by the sight of the blood running down my arm.

The light outside my window was fading, but my arm seemed to glow in the dark. I dragged the blade across it with varying levels of force-sometimes the cuts only stung, and sometimes they burned. I didn't care. What mattered was that I could *feel* them.

I woke up to gray light streaming across my face. Blinking, I sat up in bed. I didn't remember going to sleep, or even getting into bed for that matter. I didn't remember anything, in fact, until I tried to move my arm.

It was stuck to my side.

Shit, Harmony.

I pulled back my sheets to find that they were glued together with blood in some places. Rory's keys were lying beside my pillow, the knife blade still open. It was a miracle I hadn't stabbed myself in the eye while I slept.

As quietly as possible, I slid out of bed and snuck down the hall. It was early, not even six am, and I could see through my mother's partially opened door that the two of them were still asleep.

The bathroom seemed unreasonably bright compared to my dimly illuminated bedroom, and I blinked several times before getting to work. I rinsed the blood thoroughly from the knife blade with soap and cold water, then scrubbed it until it shone. My arm was a slightly more pragmatic affair, I had to peel several fibers from my t shirt off of it before I could even assess the damage. At first glance, it was a bloody, ruined mess. I knew from experience, however, that once I'd cleaned it it wouldn't look nearly as bad.

The skin stung as I scrubbed it hard under the cold water, splattering pink stains around the basin of the sink. I watched the tainted water gather around the drain before disappearing with an unappetizing gurgle. Then finally, I held up my arm. Pink scratches covered the surface from wrist to elbow, and I ran my finger over the raw skin, feeling bump after bump. They'd be gone in a few weeks, I knew, and they wouldn't even scar over. Maybe ten of them would last, but only five were really deep. One was still bleeding as I looked at it that morning, turning my hand over so the fresh droplets of blood could land in the sink. One, two, three drops. The fourth one beaded on the edge of the cut but never fell.

I didn't feel disappointed in myself or ashamed for having broken a nearly five week streak. Maybe I should have. Instead, there was only slight annoyance. Summer was the hardest time to hide cuts, when it was often too hot to wear long sleeves inconspicuously. *Seriously, how stupid can you get, Harmony?*

Whatever. I felt a little sick, and a little light headed too, so I figured I'd dwell on it later. After triple checking that everything in the bathroom was undisturbed, I crept down the stairs and returned Rory's keys to the table. *Had they been on the table or the counter?* I was too tired to remember, and I still had to change my sheets.

I went through the steps of this process robotically, slipping from room to room without ever really stopping to assess what I was doing. I guess looking back I can see that I was beginning to lose my mind, but at the time all I could think about was going back to bed.

I finally did, sliding between clean sheets and falling back asleep immediately. I didn't dream, and when I woke up again it was almost 2pm.

Only then did I think to check my phone. One missed message from Alana, from three hours earlier.

Alana: Hey Harm. Idk what got into Noah he can be such a dick. Hope u ok.

I typed back. I'm fine.

Then I put my phone down and fell back asleep. I'd never felt so tired in my life.

By the time school started, most of the cuts were gone, as I knew they'd be. The ones that weren't had scabbed over enough that I could successfully cover them with concealer.

I made up my mind to just stay away from him, to stay away from all of them. He'd been right, anyway. I didn't belong there.

I managed to go through almost the entire first day without running into him. Instead, I ate lunch with Jessica, Taylor, Maya and Laina, the student council girls I'd met the year before. They chattered along about their summers and all the times they'd hung out, and I nodded and laughed with them in all the right places. Anyone watching would have guessed that I was fully engaged in their conversations, and that I was happy to be. It would have crossed no one's mind that I was actually sneaking glances around the cafeteria, gym, halls and classrooms, looking for dark eyes and a Lakers sweatshirt, because I wasn't.

Of course, whether I was looking or not, I did see him. At the end of the day, getting on the bus, I overheard someone call his name.

Before I could tell myself not to, I turned around. I felt like after so much anticipation and dread he should have looked different, somehow, like seeing him should have been more of an event. But no, he was just Noah, just like he always had been, hanging on to the straps of his backpack and wearing dark jeans and a purple t shirt that didn't match his J's, the same pair he'd worn the day I first met him. His hair was longer, in curls that fell over his forehead, but not so long that I couldn't see his eyes beneath it.

See them staring at me.

His smile, which had been wide a moment before while he joked with his friends, softened, and he wet his lips, ducking his head. I don't know if i was glaring at him or not, but from the way his eyes dimmed, I definitely wasn't smiling. I don't know how I felt- angry or sad or confused. But I did feel *something*, looking at him. I felt for the first time in a month, since I'd spent a night slashing my own wrists open.

His eyes were like that stupid knife, cutting in to me, and I was bleeding right there in the middle of the bus loop. I hated him then, for being the only thing that could remind me that I was still alive, that I could still feel pain. More than that, though, I hated myself, for somehow having let him in to an extent where seeing him was the only thing that made me feel like living, but the distance between us was the main thing that made me want to die. I hated myself because I knew I was the cause for the distance, because I should have run up to him and pushed him into the street and screamed at him for betraying me, for being such an asshole, but I didn't. I just stared at him. And I turned away when he said my name.

I ran from the only thing I wanted; to feel, to feel anything, because I knew he didn't feel anything back. I ran away, just like I always did.

Go back, Harmony.

But I didn't.

Say something, Harmony.

But I wouldn't.

Be normal, Harmony.

But I wasn't.

Live, Harmony.

But I couldn't.

I hated myself and I hated myself and I hated myself.

PART THREE

Arms

"The red one." Hannah popped her gum in a sticky pink bubble that I assume smelt like strawberries, but I was only guessing because she was 2,000 miles away.

"Are you sure?" I held up the red dress, a hand me down that she had given me before she moved away. It was pretty, with a scoop neck and long sleeves, but it was tight. "Isn't it kinda… slutty?"

"Oh my god, Harmony." her voice was tinny and hollow through facetime, but the exasperation in it came through loud and clear. "Would you just live a little? Also I'd appreciate it if you refrained from the use of the word 'slutty' when referring to clothing that I once wore."

"Sorry." I smirked, and kicked out of my jeans, tugging the fabric of the dress over my head. I trusted Hannah more than I trusted myself when it came to fashion, a fact that she well knew. She could have told me to wear a burlap sack over my head, and I probably would have been talked into it.

"Isn't the dance tonight anyway? You don't exactly have a lot of time for indecision. I don't understand how you can get away with leaving everything to the last minute all the time. I'd have panic attacks something awful."

I shrugged, frowning at my reflection as I applied makeup. "I didn't wanna go to the stupid dance anyway. It's not like I have anyone to go with, and I'll have to walk home."

"Christ Harm, could you get anymore depressing? It's *homecoming*, everybody goes to homecoming. And don't even make some smart ass comment about how you're 'not everybody'. You're *some*body, somebody who's going to this damn dance."

I let her rattle on, she was the reason I'd even considered going to the dance in the first place. Taylor, Jessica and Maya were going, and while they'd pouted when I said I didn't have plans to, I could tell they weren't really that upset. Alana and Gio were going, too, and so were Lexi and Jaideson, along with the rest of their group. Along with Noah.

It was October, and I'd managed to avoid him all month. I told myself that I didn't wanna see him, even while I was looking for him. I told myself that I chose to go to classes the long way because I liked the walk, even as I was passing him in the hallway. And I told myself that I went to every football game because I was socializing, even while my eyes followed him across the field.

I don't know what I was doing- I wanted him to see me avoiding him so that he would come up to me, but he didn't. He didn't care, and it killed me a little everyday.

So no, I didn't want to go to homecoming, at the same time that I was desperate for someone to convince me to do just that. When Hannah had asked about the dance a few weeks earlier, I'd been successfully evasive enough to spark her insistence in my attending.

So here we were, the night of the dance, and she was trying to muster some enthusiasm into me. I ran my hands down my sides, looking at myself in the mirror. The dress looked ok, I thought. It matched my hair, though I wasn't sure if that was a good or bad thing. My makeup was how I always did it- just heavy enough that I couldn't recognize myself, but probably not very becoming. Even my shoes were a travesty- converse. I was terrible at being a girl. I was terrible at being anything.

"Harmony." I'd forgotten that Hannah was still on the phone, but from her tone of voice, she knew exactly what I was thinking. I bit my lip, looking at my reflection again. I was nervous, nervous that I was drawing too much attention to myself and he would notice me, and nervous that I wasn't drawing enough attention, and he wouldn't notice at all.

"Are you ok?" Her voice had lost it's usual dramatic air, and revealed what I suspected often existed beneath the surface. Worry. Worry and confusion. She was my best friend, and even she didn't understand me.

I forced a smile onto my face. "I'm fine."

I'm fine.

Rory offered to drive me but I wanted to walk, slipping out the door in the midst of my mother's rebukes on my outfit.

The school was already crowded by the time I came around the corner, packed with girls in dresses much more revealing than mine, and boys who looked like they were already stoned, for the most part. The football players were easy to distinguish, they were still high off their win earlier in the night. I could see them rough housing by the north entrance and immediately veered toward the other side of the school.

"Harmony, you made it." Jess bounced up to me, beaming. Her six foot boyfriend, Nate, maybe, followed in tow, holding her purse.

"Yea, I figured I might as well." I shrugged, taking in Jess from head to toe. "You look great." and she did, in a sparkly midnight blue dress that accentuated her breasts and flared out just under her ribs, to end mid thigh. It went perfectly with her thick curls and bronze skin, and when she turned her face, I could see her eye shadow matched perfectly. She'd obviously spent hours picking out her outfit, and I suddenly felt even more insecure in mine.

"Thank you!" she squealed, clasping her hands. I smiled. Hannah would have loved Jess. "I'll see you inside, kay honey? They've got cake and soda, we'll grab some later, ok?" she squeezed my hand and then grabbed Nate's arm, dragging him inside.

I watched them until they were lost in the crowd, then bent to tie my shoe. Finally, when I knew I could put off going in no longer, I took a deep breath, and walked inside.

People. People everywhere. Girls squealing about how cute each other's outfits were, guys giving each other daps and congratulating the football players on the game. People were already dancing, the lights were already down, it already smelt like pot.

"Harmony. Didn't think you'd show up." Mr. Waiter was smiling at me curiously as he took my ticket.

"I didn't think I'd see you here either." I replied. A boy shoved past me, and my left side banged into the wall.

"Ah, well, someone has to keep you guys under control. Between you and me though," he smiled, "there are other places I'd rather be on a Friday night. These dances can get a little rough. I wouldn't have placed it as your scene."

"I'm trying to live a little." I shouted over the music without thinking.

"I suppose in high school this is living." He stamped my ticket and handed it back. "Have a good night and be safe, kiddo."

I nodded and forced myself into the gym. Immediately, I was swallowed by the crowd, only surfacing in bits and pieces when I ran into Taylor and Maya and swayed along while they lost their minds to Bruno Mars, and when Gio, who was clearly drunk out of his mind, grabbed me in a hug so intense that I was lifted off my feet.

"Are you having fun?!" he shouted when he finally put me down, barely coherent.

I raised an eyebrow. "Sure, G. Where's Alana? Aren't you guys here together?"

"What? Oh, yea. Yea, she's my girl. She and Lexi went to go score some grass from her locker though. They should be back soon. You tryna stick around to smoke?"

"Nah, I'm good, thanks though."

"Oh yea, I forgot." He grinned and leaned closer to me, so far that I was afraid he was about to fall over. "You don't smoke."

I took a step back. He was probably too out of it to be making a reference to the summer intentionally, but I was immediately reminded of it.

"Devante was looking for you." He continued. He was obviously trying to convey something, with his smirk and raised eyebrows, but it had gone over my head.

I left, thinking maybe I'd get some fresh air. It wasn't a terrible time, but I was beginning to wish I had just stayed home. I was headed toward the gym door, knowing I'd be locked out as soon as it closed behind me and secretly relieved that I'd have an excuse to go home, when I walked right into someone. Pot, sweat, ranch, Old Spice, and boy, all diluted by a warm, soft, clean scent that instantly made me feel safe.

"Woah woah. Harmony?" I felt his hands fall gently on my arms. Instinctively, I turned my face away.

He took a step back, still holding me in place carefully while he looked me over. Looking back, I realize that he might have been holding me up. "Why do you look so nice?" His face was scrunched, like he'd forgotten we were at a dance, like he'd just run into me at Kmart. He didn't sound like he was paying me a compliment, he sounded genuinely curious.

"It's a dance. My mom said I had to look nice." My voice came out flat and monotonous, the exact opposite of how I actually felt.

"Well," he shrugged, finally letting his arms fall. My skin burned where he'd touched it. "I think you always look nice."

"If only you were my mother." I tried to side step him, though suddenly my motor skills were not much better than Gio's.

"Are you still mad at me?"

I stopped. Not because of what he'd said, but because of how he'd said it. He sounded... empty. He didn't sound like Noah.

He sounded like me.

"You never apologized." I tried to say it coolly, but I'm sure my voice cracked. *Leave, Harmony. Leave now before you fuck this up even worse.*

I tried, but he grabbed my left wrist, and my cuts stung like hell. I jerked it back.

"Dammit, Harmony." His voice was sharp, and I tensed immediately. My back was still to him, but I could hear him sigh. "You've been ignoring me all year, Harm. When the hell was I supposed to apologize?"

I didn't answer. I didn't want him to be right, but I knew he was. If he was right then I couldn't be mad, or at least not as mad. And I really didn't want to find out what would replace my anger.

He came up behind me and touched my wrist again. "Harmony." I breathed in response. "Dance with me?"

"I don't dance." I whispered.

"And I don't apologize, but if you dance with me I might."

I couldn't help it, I had to laugh at that. "To this song?" It was Just a Dream by Nelly, and people were going crazy.

"Sure." he shrugged, returning my grin. I had to admit that I'd missed it. His whole face was arguably above average, but his smile was extraordinary. It stretched wide enough that I could see all his teeth, including one gold one in the back, and it lit up his eyes even brighter than usual. "I like this song."

"So do I," I admitted. "Which means I'll probably drive you crazy by singing all the words. I don't dance, Noah." I looked at him apologetically, though every ounce of my body was screaming at me. He made some exasperated sound in the back of his throat and rolled his eyes, going to turn away. Without thinking, I grabbed his hand.

He stopped, and looked down at our hands before looking back at me. His face was impossible to read. I took a breath. "But I do want to talk to you. Find me later?"

He nodded, his lips pursed, and disappeared back into the crowd. Only after he left did I realize that he had bent his fingers around mine.

Whether he meant to find me later or not, I don't know, but I did see him again that night.

The dance ended at 9:30, and by then it was undeniably pretty cold out, not to mention dark and foggy. The perfect fall night for a girl to walk home alone in a party dress.

It was only a mile or so walk, and while I knew I should have just called Rory and asked him to come get me, I was feeling unusually stubborn. I'd said I was going to walk home and so I would. I'd said I didn't need a jacket and so I didn't. I *was* secretly grateful for my converse for the first time, even I knew I never would have managed that walk in a pair of the stilletos a few of the other girls were wearing.

"Hey, million dollar baby." I had just started on my way when Noah's voice found me through the crowd of drunk and danced out teenagers ambling into the parking lot, and he jogged over to me. "Let me use your phone?"

I dug it out of my bag and handed it to him. While he dialed I took the opportunity to look him over for the first time. Dark jeans and new Jordans, and a charcoal gray button down with the sleeves rolled up. And, of course, his Lakers sweatshirt. It occurred to me how nice he looked in long sleeves, especially when they were rolled up. Like he was getting ready to do something important. He looked much younger.

"You never go anywhere without that fucking hoodie, do you?"

"It's comfy." He smiled. "One sec." He put the phone to his ear and chewed his lip. I had nothing to do but eavesdrop, and after all, it was my damn phone.

"Hey, Momma. Yeah, no, yeah it was fine. Sure. Can you come pick me up?" there was a long pause, and he sucked in his cheeks, kicking a rock into the gutter. "Yeah, I know. *Yes.* Jesus, woman. No, nothing. I didn't say nothing." He looked at me. "Hold up one sec." Putting his hand over the phone he leaned toward me. "You tryna give me a ride?"

"I can't." I told him. "I'm walking."

"Where you walking?"

I pointed.

"Alone?"

I shrugged.

"Bet, okay." he put the phone back up to his ear. "Look Momma I'm gonna walk with a friend. Yeah, yeah sure. I promise. Okay. Cool, thanks. Love you." The line had already clicked dead.

He looked at the black screen for a moment, his expression indecipherable.

"Noah?" I asked carefully.

He glanced up as though he had forgotten he wasn't alone. Quickly, he grinned, and handed the phone back. I raised an eyebrow. "You're walking with me?"

"Well, I'm not gonna let you walk alone." He rolled his eyes as though it were the most obvious thing in the world, then turned and waved to some kids from the football team as they drove by.

"I'm perfectly capable of walking by myself." I informed him. We were supposed to be arguing, and staying mad at him was going to be a lot harder when he was walking me home.

"Harmony. Come on." He glanced at me and raised an eyebrow, but his eyes were dead serious. He had already started walking, so there was nothing for me to do but follow.

We walked in silence until we were out of the parking lot, broken only when we passed people he knew, which was quite often, and he had to stop to give them daps and hugs and those complicated handshakes that boys do. It felt a little like walking home with a celebrity. Noah was just one of those people that everyone knew, that everyone called by their first and last name, that everyone wanted to be friends with. His smile was contagious, his hugs were irresistible, and when he was in a bad mood, *everyone* knew to stay clear. He could change the atmosphere of a room just by walking into it. He was everything that I wasn't, but for some reason, there he was, walking me home.

"So." he said finally, once we were past the school, and the shouts and car horns were fading into the background. I lived two neighborhoods from the high school, which meant that part of the walk would take us down a main road. Just then, however, we were still on a side street. It was dark, it was quiet, and we were as alone as we ever had been.

"So." I repeated.

He sighed, and scratched the back of his neck. "Look, that day... I was high. I was in a bad mood. I don't really remember what I said but I know it wasn't good. I feel bad, Harm. The looks you been giving me make me feel like it was a lot worse than I remember. I'm sorry, okay?"

I didn't say anything. If I'd been giving him dirty looks I'd done so subconsciously, I didn't think he had noticed me at all since the school year started. It occured to me, however, that he wasn't the only one who had acted like an asshole that day, and so if he was going out of his way to apologize then I probably should too.

"Well, I didn't exactly greet you very nicely either. Making fun of your girlfriend, or whatever."

"Girlfriend?" he wrinkled his nose. "Who, Gianna? She's just a girl I hooked up with a couple times over the summer, I think she's Lexi's cousin or something. I haven't even talked to her since school started."

Something in my chest loosened. *Brilliant, Harmony, you're relieved that they were just having casual sex and getting high together. This is really what's been bothering you? Jesus, get a grip.*

As usual, my lack of response only prompted him to keep talking.

"I don't care about what you said to her, that was pretty funny, actually."

"So then why?" I heard myself say. "If you weren't mad at me then why'd you act like such a dick? That was out of line, Noah, and you know it."

He sighed, and for once he was quiet. Out of the corner of my eye I could see him biting his nails, a quirk I'd noticed a couple times before. He was uneasy, which was unusual for him.

"Why, Noah?" I softened my voice, knowing I'd be more likely to get answers if I wasn't yelling at him.

"Because I didn't want you to see me. Not like that." He ran his hands through his hair before shoving them in his back pockets. "Everyone in this fucking school sees me how they want to see me- a jock, a stoner, a deadbeat, a fuck boy, whatever. People know me by the things I've done, or the things they *think* I've done, not by who I really am. But you… I don't know. You look at me like you don't care what people say about me, even if you know they're right. You kinda give me a chance to be something else for a change. I didn't wanna lose that."

By the time he'd finished, his voice was raspy, and I heard him swallow. He was embarrassed, maybe, or tired, or anxious, or all three. He was perfectly imperfect- not a celebrity or a deadbeat or anything else. He was just a kid, a kid who threw chairs when he got mad and who bit his nails and who could light up a room the minute he walked into it.

I knew that this time I'd have to say something.

"How do you see yourself?" I asked. "What do you want to be?"

"Professional athlete." He was answering a question that I hadn't asked, and he knew it, but I decided to give him a break and go along with it.

"Basketball?" He nodded. It may have been football season, and he was certainly capable on the field, but I had seen him play ball the previous winter, and there was no doubt that he belonged on the court.

"That sounds attainable. What's plan B?"

"Mailman." he said, without skipping a beat. He kicked a can into the gutter as we passed it. If it had been anyone but Noah, I would have been sure he was kidding, but with him you never knew.

"You may be the last person on the planet I'd trust to handle my mail." I was hoping to get him to laugh, to relax a little, and it worked. We were quiet again for a while, we'd turned on to the main street and city noises filled the silence between us until I mustered the courage to speak again, to say what I'd wanted to for months.

"Do you remember that day in gym, when you said that you feel like you look at yourself and you only see what other people see?"

His voice was quiet when he answered. "Yeah."

"Well," I hoped that he couldn't hear me sucking in my breath. "I wish you would look at yourself and see what I see."

"Why?" I could hear something strained in his voice. "What do you see?"

I stopped walking and turned to him, as if I needed to look at him to be reminded. "I see a lot of potential." I told him. He had stopped too. "You're an incredibly talented athlete, Noah. You're cute, and bright, and intuitive. You got a way with people that I have *never* seen before. You're a good kid but you got a mean streak and you gotta learn how to control it. You got so much going for you, but your head's too far stuck up your ass for you to see that."

His eyes widened and he opened his mouth slightly, then closed it. For a minute he just stared at me, and I forced myself to stare back, stupidly defiant.

And this, Harmony, is why you keep your damn mouth shut. You never know what you're going to say until you're already through saying it.

Then he turned and we kept walking, as though we'd never stopped. He was quiet for a while longer, and I began to hear a dog barking up ahead.

There was a smile in his voice when he finally said, "You think I'm cute?"

"Oh please, Noah. You know you are." I responded curtly, but I snuck a glance at him. I was hoping he'd retained more than that one stupid comment. One look told me he had heard everything that I'd said, he just didn't know how to respond to anything else.

I was going to say something else, I don't know what, when a car drove by, so close to the curb that I could smell the weed on the passenger's breath when he leaned out the window and whistled. "Okay, baby!" one of the kids yelled. "How much for you to let *me* walk you home?"

They broke up into howls of laughter and roared off, at least 20 miles over the speed limit. I rolled my eyes and pulled my dress down in the back, then glanced at my chest to see if there was anyway I could cover myself more.

Noah's eyes were on the skin below my collarbone, as if he'd just noticed it was exposed, his jaw set and his mouth a thin line. Without speaking, he pulled off his sweatshirt and thrust it toward me. It wasn't that cold and we both knew it, but I put it on anyway.

"You know, it bothers you a lot more than it bothers me." I said gently, after I was relatively confident that he wasn't going to explode.

"Yeah, well," his voice was tight, and he stared straight ahead. "It should bother you more."

"I'm used to it, it's not that big a deal."

"Yes, it is, okay?" He turned to me finally, and I was relieved to see his face soften. "It looks good on you." He pulled the hood out in the back, and I tried to hide my shiver when his fingers brushed against my neck.

"It smells like you." I said, without thinking. *Christ.*

Luckily, he just laughed. "Well, I'd be worried if it smelled like anybody else."

I was about to return his smile when something suddenly crashed against the fence on my right. It was a huge dog, seemingly out of nowhere, and it was barking like crazy. Noah jumped off the curb, pushing me behind him. "Holy shit!" he yelped.

I laughed, over my initial shock. The dog wasn't as big as I'd originally thought, and it was chained up inside the fence. Noah, on the other hand, was still chalk white.

"Noah Andrade, are you afraid of dogs?" I was trying not to smile.

"No." He breathed heavily. "I am not *afraid of dogs.*"

I glanced down at my arm, which he still held in a death grip, and raised an eyebrow. "You're afraid of dogs."

"Why, do you have one?" He looked so genuinely worried that I couldn't hold back my laughter anymore.

"Shut up." He rolled his eyes. "Dogs can be mean."

"Not if they're chained behind a fence, Noah!"

"Whatever." He crossed his arms, trying to be upset, but I could see his eyes were bright.

"That's for real kinda funny, you know, cause of the way that you act."

"What do you mean?"

"You know… you kinda act like a puppy." I scratched the back of my neck. *Jesus, Harmony.*

"A puppy." He repeated. I could hear the smile in his voice.

Oh well. It's not like I could take it back now. "Yeah, always jumping all over people all hyper and stuff, wanting attention." It had sounded reasonable in my head, but anyone hearing me say it would have thought I was special for sure.

But Noah... well, he wasn't anyone. When I looked at him, he was smiling so wide his eyes had almost disappeared. He tugged at my hair gently and leaned over to bury his face in my neck. I laughed.

"Yeah, exactly like that."

His breath was warm down the collar of my dress when he laughed before pulling away. "See this?" he touched the scar on his cheek, which I'd wondered about before. "My mom's boyfriend had a rottweiler. I was five."

I pretended to study the scar, just as an excuse to look at him. "I knew you didn't get that cut in a fight." Which was what I'd heard.

"Nah, when people ask, that's what I tell them though." He shrugged, but there was an underlying tone in his voice that I struggled to identify for a moment. Girls, that's what he was trying to say. That's what he told girls. In bed.

I could feel him looking at me, trying to read me the same way I tried to read him, so I shook it off. "Did you piss it off?"

"No! I was minding my own buisness, coloring or some shit, and the thing fucking attacked me!"

"Okay, okay." I laughed. "If you got ptsd or whatever I guess you get a pass. Most dogs aren't like that though. Not if you take good care of them."

"Yeah, well." His eyes dimmed. "I don't know how well taken care of that dog was."

Not thinking was becoming a theme for me that night, and it persisted when I reached out to touch his wrist. He slid his hand into mine and squeezed it briefly, his eyes closed. "Was he mean?" I asked quietly, and he knew I wasn't asking about the dog.

In answer, he pulled up his shirt and walked over to the nearest streetlight, in front of the 7/11. He looked down the street, his face expressionless, while I took in his chest. I'd only seen him shirtless from a distance, and up close I noticed things I hadn't before. 10 years worth of muscles from football built into his stomach. A tattoo that looked like it had been done in someone's garage on his left side- a cross. And on his right side, two small scars. His skin was such a warm shade of brown that they stood out like dimes in a sea of pennies, just the size of...

"Cigarettes." Somehow, I'd known it before I'd even seen them. He nodded, still staring back toward the dog. Without remembering having decided to do it, I reached out my hand hesitantly.

He glanced down, and his face tightened. I waited, not sure if he wanted me to touch him. Not sure if *I* wanted to touch him. "It's okay." He said finally.

I ran my finger across his skin, feeling the differentiation of the scar tissue. It was thinner, rougher, like crumpled tissue paper. Just as warm, though.

Something occurred to me suddenly, as I traced the imperfections on his stomach. Out of nowhere, the thought entered my mind that no one could smile as much as he did, and not be faking it at least half the time. A crack ran through my heart at the realization, and I wished more than anything that my fingertip could erase the scars on his skin. I wanted to cry. I just wanted to hold him, actually, but he wasn't mine to hold.

The thought made me feel even more like crying.

"How old were you?"

"Six."

"Do you remember it?" I hadn't moved my hand from his chest and he didn't ask me to.

"I remember that it hurt like hell." He said, "I remember waking up in the middle of the night to ice it, so I wouldn't have to tell my mom." My silence told him what I thought about that, and he sighed. "I put my mother through so much shit, Harmony. Between me and my brothers... poor lady can't catch a break. And this guy... I don't know. He seemed to make her happy. I didn't wanna mess that up for her, too."

"Noah..." I pulled my hand back and he shivered, as though realizing for the first time that he was practically shirtless at 10pm in October. He let his shirt fall, and we kept walking.

"I honestly doubt that your mother cared more about her sex life than the fact that her boyfriend was putting out his cigarettes on her six year old." I may have been too harsh, but if he was gonna open up to me then he deserved to know how I really felt, too. "She loves you, Noah."

"She never says it."

"Bullshit." I told him. "What did she say to you on the phone tonight?"

"What?"

"When you called her. What did she say?" We had turned into my neighborhood, I could see Rory's Kia parked outside my house at the end of the street.

"She said she wasn't gonna come pick me up."

"And?" I pressed.

"She said I better have my ass home by 11." He hesitated. "And she made me promise I wouldn't walk home alone."

"Exactly."

"It's not the same thing. She hasn't told me she loves me in… I can't even remember how long."

"Noah, listen to me. There's more than one way to say 'I love you.' Like, you ever been in the car with your momma, and like maybe she's mad at you, 'cause you did something stupid or whatever. And she's yelling at you, 'cause moms always yell at you when they got you in the car and you can't run away, right?" He grinned, nodding. I could tell part of him was desperate to know what I was gonna say. "And then she looks over at you and goes 'would you put your fucking seatblet on?!'"

He nodded again. "Yeah, sure. Sounds like my ride to school this morning. Why, though?"

We were two houses away from mine, and I could see the kitchen light on. I stopped again to look at him. "She's saying that she loves you when she says that. Every time she says 'be careful' or 'are you hungry?' or 'be home by 11.' Everytime she tells you that she's in your corner, that she's got your back no matter what, even when you're driving her crazy, she's saying she loves you. Maybe she doesn't always have time to remember to say the words, but I guarantee you she still tells you everyday. And if you get home tonight and you find her waiting up for you, you'll know she's saying it again."

I finished talking and looked up to see him staring at me in awe. I was getting better at reading him, and I was surprised to see that his eyes were full of gratitude. I hadn't thought I was saying anything that was gonna reassure him or really even make him feel better. It had never occurred to me that anything I said had any effect on him at all. Until that moment, I had thought I was just a sounding board for him to bounce his thoughts off of whenever he found time to talk to me. I realized though, that night, that maybe he had told me things that he wouldn't have told just anybody. Maybe, I meant something to him after all. Definitely not as much as he meant to me, but maybe something.

Maybe.

"This is my house." I broke the silence, pointing to my bedroom window. Pointing to the roof.

His eyes followed my hand and he nodded.

"Did you wanna come in? My mom's boyfriend could probably drive you home. I don't have a dog, I promise."

He smiled and shook his head. "Nah, that's okay. I don't live too far from here, actually. I can walk you to your yard, though."

I nodded, and we cut across the grass until we were standing under the fire escape by my window. He looked up and smiled. "Is that your room?" The window was plastered with stickers.

"Yeah. I can climb onto the roof by standing on the edge of the window sill." I didn't add what my thoughts on top of the roof usually were. He looked thoughtful, and maybe a little sad. For one irrational moment, I was sure that he knew what I thought about while I was sitting up there. But that was impossible.

Stands With a Fist slunk across the yard and brushed against my ankles, meowing. He looked indignantly at Noah, as though he did not belong standing in our front yard, which was true. He didn't belong in my life at all.

"Hey, cat." he bent to scratch the cat behind his ears. Stands With a Fist immediately changed his attitude now that he was getting attention, purring and swishing his tail.

"Oh please, don't encourage him. That cat is full of himself enough as it is."

Noah laughed and straightened up. "I like cats okay. Their scratches are nothing compared to a dog."

"I don't think they hurt at all."

"Of course you don't." His eyes were serious.

I swallowed. "Text me when you get home, okay?"

"Yes ma'am." He smiled, and took a step closer to me, closing the distance between us, something I never would have done. He was always the one to close the distance.

I put my head on his shoulder and wrapped my arms around his waist, tighter than I ever had before. He didn't seem surprised, his hold on me was just as hard. We stood like that for I don't know how long, not saying anything. He always hugged me when we met or left each other, looping his arms over mine and tucking his head into my neck. This time, though, I knew that the scars on my arm were pressed against the ones on his side.

"You know, I meant it, Harm. You look really pretty tonight. I mean, you never look bad." he pulled back slowly, sliding his hand under my hair to cup my cheek. The yard was dark, the nearest streetlight was behind us, and the sky was pitch black, but his eyes still shone like they were coated in clear nail polish.

"I forgive you, Noah." I whispered into his palm.

"Why?" His face scrunched up, like he didn't think that I should have.

"Because." I took a deep breath. "You're my friend. That means I got your back no matter what."

His eyes had never been so bright, and his thumb was rubbing against my lips. *If you ever want to kiss him, Harmony, to have a chance with him at all, you gotta do it now.*

But I didn't. "Goodnight, Superman." I whispered, just to make him smile. I squeezed his hand briefly, then turned and walked away. I didn't look back until I was inside, with the door closed behind me. Only then did I realize I was still wearing his sweatshirt.

I couldn't have kissed him. I wanted him more than I'd ever wanted anything, but I couldn't have done it. We were friends, real friends, at least that night we were, I couldn't deny that. But he was so special, he was so unlike anyone I'd ever met before, and he was broken enough as it was. I couldn't have bared to risk breaking him any more. He deserved somebody who lit up the room, just like he did. He deserved somebody who had put up with the same amount of shit that he had, and who still lived her fullest everyday, just like he did. He deserved someone who didn't voluntarily get her scars. He deserved somebody better than me.

I pulled off his sweatshirt before going into my mom's room, where she was up reading, and told her that the dance had been fun. When she asked how I'd gotten home, I said I'd walked with Maya. We said goodnight, and I escaped to my bedroom. The window was closed and I didn't want to risk opening it, so I just washed my face, brushed my hair out, and put on my pajamas. Before I got into bed, I pulled his sweatshirt back over my head. I couldn't help it.

I was almost asleep when my phone buzzed, a little after 11.

Noah: i'm home. my mom was waiting up. sweet dreams, million dollar baby.

I smiled, and didn't respond.

PART FOUR

Keep Breathing

I wish that I could tell you that night was a game changer for me. I wish I could say that my life turned around, that I got better, that I told Noah how I felt, that we ended up together. I wish I could tell you that was how this story ended. But you already know that it's not.

This story ends nine months after homecoming of my sophomore year, and if you can't guess how, then you clearly haven't been paying good attention. I don't know why I'll even bother telling you about the events of those nine months, I don't know if there's a point. I can't even tell you that what happened that year was what ended my life, because it really wasn't. I'm the only thing to blame for that.

I want to be able to tell you that this story is about Noah, because a story about him and about how easy it was to fall in love with him would be a story worth telling, and a story worth listening to. Unfortunately, this is my story, and it's not one that's worth much of anything.

But I'll tell it to you anyway. There's only nine months left, afterall.

If I were to title each remaining section of this story by what happened in it, there would be eight, and they would look like this:

1. My mother's rough wake up call
2. Crisis in California
3. Cameron, Joel, and Jared Andrade
4. The day I spent convinced that Noah was dead
5. The roof, part one
6. Noah's unintentional attempt to ruin his life, and how I got in the way of that
7. A boy who did one thing right
8. The roof, again

When I write it like that, it seems so simple. The most eventful months of my life, chalked up to eight bullet points. 53 words. How important it all seemed then, and how little it seems to matter now.

But I'm getting ahead of myself. I'm telling you parts of my story that haven't happened yet, and while I don't think there's anyway to tell this story right, there are about a million ways to tell it wrong.

So let's just start at the beginning, it's as good a place as any. Let's start with my mother, and how I managed to ruin her life before I even got around to ruining mine.

It started two weeks after homecoming, on an otherwise uneventful Tuesday night. The lack of other extraordinary occurrences only served to amplify the days main event, both to me, and to the rest of the neighborhood. The fight.

I don't know what they were fighting about, money, probably, that force that consumes the lives and minds of every human person after a certain age. Don't get me wrong, they bickered often, small arguments over the inconsequential daily ups and downs of life- how she had washed his pants while his wallet was still in them, making him an hour late for work, which he'd spent fuming in front of the washing machine, watching his jeans spin innocently around. Or maybe he'd forgotten to put out the hamburger to defrost, and she had to waste money on take out because there was no other food in the damn house and we couldn't just sit around and starve, could we?

Every once in a while, however, they got into real fights. Fights with screaming and slamming doors and horrible accusations and ultimatums, fights that always ended with him packing his bags and storming out the front door, swearing that he was "done for real this time, Courtney. Done and not coming back." That night was one of the worst.

He got home late, one, maybe, and she was waiting up. She was already in a bad mood, she'd snapped at me over dinner, and she was just looking for an excuse to be mad. Something set her off, beer on his breath, probably, and that was it. I lay in bed, wide awake, staring at the ceiling while I listened to them scream at each other like they'd forgotten anyone else was in the house, which they probably had.

He got sarcastic when he was mad, (specifically when he was mad and drunk) accusing her of thinking she was so much smarter than him, and if she was so fucking smart and he was so fucking stupid then why did she bother staying with him, huh? Then she had to respond with some equally smart ass remark about how she needed him to "even her out" or something like that, and he would lose his shit. He reminded me on those occasions of Judd Nelson in the Breakfast Club, in the scene where he screams "FUCK YOU!" to the principal so loud that they have to adjust the sound of the recording.

If I'm making it sound like I blamed either of them, that's not my intention. I didn't hate Rory by any means, he had never in the 10 years that he'd been around *ever* laid a hand on her, or cheated on her, or anything. He was a decent guy, and like I've said already, he and I got along pretty well most of the time. And of course I couldn't hate my mother, not because of some stupid notion that I owed her undying devotion because I'd existed inside of her for nine months, but because she was a good mom as often as she remembered to be, and at the end of the day I loved her very much. I loved both of them, and they loved each other, I really do believe that. Love was not the problem in my house. The problem was that we were three people (and one cat) who lived together and ate together and loved each other, but we could never quite manage to be a family. I guess in part the reason was that in a family you're obligated to stay even when you don't want to, and in my house, no one felt an obligation to do anything.

He left that night, finally, around 2:30. I went to my window and watched him throw his gym bag into his car, slamming the door so loud I would have sworn it had woken the whole neighborhood, if their fight hadn't already. I put my hand on the glass and said his name, and he paused, looking up at my window as though he had heard me.

I waved, but my light was off, and he couldn't see me. He shook his head and slammed his fist on the hood of his car. He looked angry, he looked defeated, he looked like he didn't know what to do next. It was a little like looking in a mirror.

After watching him throw open the door and go roaring off down the block, I went to the door of my room. There was no need to check on my mom, I knew what she was doing. Still, I waited for another half an hour before opening my window. It was 3am, it was a school night, it was freezing, and it was pitch dark out, but I pulled myself onto the fire escape, my bare feet slipping on the railing, and felt around until my hands reached the outcropping of the roof.

I hoisted myself up, and I had almost made it, when my left foot slipped off the back of the railing, and suddenly I was dangling 50 feet above the ground, with only my fingers pressing into the shingles above my head.

I looked down, toward where I knew the ground was, and saw my body lying there, broken from the inside out. No one would even find it for another three hours, at least, not until it was already stiff and cold and frosted with dew. No one would ever see me warm again.

I realized that if I fell that night, it would occur to no one that it could have been accidental. No one would ever assume that I had had no intention of killing myself that night, that I had just been climbing onto the roof at 3am to sit there. Then again, was there ever a time when I sat on the roof that I didn't think about stepping off?

The wind pushed against my back, and I felt my fingers begin to slip. My arms burned with the effort to keep myself alive.

Try once.

Try once to pull yourself up. If you try once and you can't do it, then that's that.

That's that.

That's that.

I tightened my hold on the edge of the roof and heaved, swinging my legs forward. I threw one arm out and pushed hard with the other, and my elbow landed on the roof. I scrambled to get my other arm up too, and finally I felt my toe brush the railing again. My body took over it's normal routine, swinging its legs one at a time until all of it lay, panting, on top of my house. I shut my eyes, feeling the cool, innocent breathing of the earth slide across my face and down my back as I lay there. As I lay there and tried to feel scared. Tried to feel relieved. Tried to feel anything. I leaned over the side of the roof until I was staring at the ground. I saw my body there.

That's that.

I woke up feeling like shit. It was 6:30 and I had a 6:45 bus but I didn't care. A pair of clean underwear was the only article of clothing I went out of my way for that morning. I got dressed in the dark- jeans that I found on my floor, the t shirt and hoodie I slept in, then opened my bedroom door to step on a dead mouse, a perfect omen for how the rest of the day was going to go.

Stands With a Fist sat at the top of the stairs, purring and licking his whiskers. Rory never took the fucking cat with him when he left, which honestly was the main reason I knew he'd always come back.

"I hate you, you know that?" I bent to pick up Señor Squeaky by the tail, then looked up to see the cat staring at me as though he thought I was talking to him, which I hadn't been.

My mom was asleep on the couch but I didn't bother to be quiet while I walked downstairs with the cat hot on my heels. A glass that smelled like cleaning solution was tipped over by her hand, and I almost sliced my foot open trying to sidestep another broken bottle to pick it up. The living room was trashed, but it was nothing compared to the kitchen.

The bottle of Titos that she normally kept under the sink was uncapped, three quarters empty and on the counter. Sticky liquid around it and sticking to the glasses and the floor told me she had tried to mix a drink, but in the end she'd just shot the stuff straight. My mother, the 40 year old bad ass.

It took me ten minutes to get the kitchen close to it's normal standard, and even then it was sure to smell like sour mix for at least another month. There were leftovers in the fridge so I wasn't worried about her being hungry when she woke up, but I hoped she'd remember to call into work and make up some excuse, not that it really mattered. She wasn't a heavy drinker on a normal basis at all, and she rarely missed work or showed up hungover. My mother's drinking was reserved for special occasions, specifically the bad ones.

Before I left the house I noticed a last bottle of Corona, half finished on the counter. She must have opened it while she was waiting for him to come home, then abandoned it later for something stronger. I hesitated only a moment before downing the rest of it, then dropping it into the trash. I popped three Advil and two pieces of juicy fruit, grabbed my shit, and left the house. The cat followed me all the way to the bus stop, where I got on just in time, as if he was eager to get away from the house, too.

"Stupid cat." I muttered before leaning my head against the icy glass, and falling back asleep.

A freshly washed Lakers hoodie was folded in my backpack.

The next few weeks were a blur. My mom and I didn't talk about Rory or about how she'd awoke the morning after he left to find the house miraculously cleaned. We never did.

I was amazed, after the first few days of school, that no one seemed to notice that my world was slowly folding in. Without realizing it, sometime in the past few years I had managed to conceal my feelings entirely- not just from the world, but from myself. I walked around everyday and met up with Jess and smiled and listened to Alana bitch about teachers and walked to class with Noah on his good days. He'd accepted the sweatshirt back in standard Noah fashion- with an over dramatic hug and a ramble about how I hadn't needed to wash it. Other than that, though, things weren't any different between us than they had been before. He missed more school that year than the previous one, and for longer periods of time, and the gossip around the group was that his brothers were out on probation. Who these brothers were, I had still yet to find out.

I want to tell you more about those weeks in November, but they fall into the section of my life that I struggle to remember. What I do remember is being tired all the time, and having a headache that never really went away. I remember going as many as three days without eating anything, and not feeling hungry at all. I lived off coffee and ibuprofen and vodka, which in hindsight may have contributed to my constantly feeling like shit, but of course I wasn't really considering that at the time. I was depressed, and my mental health was affecting my physical state, and on some level of my remaining brain function I knew that, but I ignored it. Physically, I was dizzy, nauseous, light headed, exhausted, and a million other things. Mentally, I was nothing. I don't even think I can attribute my feelings, or lack thereof, to any surrounding circumstances or environments. Sure, my mom and Rory had fought, and the house had been quiet since he'd left, but that was nothing that hadn't happened before. I guess I was worried about Noah, and about Hannah, who's dad had been regressing, but still that was nothing new.

No, what was happening to me was entirely my own doing. Like I've said, my mother and Noah and Hannah and everyone else who had actual problems weren't the ones who were spiraling into them- I was. I felt like I was standing on the sidelines of a war, calmly slitting my own wrists.

My spiral of never ending self destruction culminated one day in early December, when, after not eating anything for 72 hours, I decided it would be a good idea to go for a run. It was freezing cold, but I wore shorts and a tank top. My arms stung like hell, not just from the merciless temperature, but from five layers of fresh cuts that lined both of them from wrist to shoulder, like dutiful soldiers in red uniform, lining up to march into the battle that I didn't bother fighting. I was running out of room on my arms and had progressed to my hips, back, and legs, areas which were more easily concealed, and a good thing too. Cutting every night meant I couldn't wait for the lacerations to scab over, and sometimes they bled right through the concealer in school. This layering of makeup over open wounds was also probably not my brightest idea, but to reiterate, I couldn't have given less of a fuck. The day before, it had occurred to me that perhaps the least conspicuous place to carve my skin was also the most conspicuous. Hiding in plain sight, you know? After all, no one would ever in a million years guess that I had taken a knife to my own face.

I suppose if you needed any more convincing that I was crazy, this has been it. I went for a run that day, pushing limbs that didn't want to move, that had no energy to move, through my own neighborhood and into unfamiliar ones. My feet pounded on the sidewalk, and with every step, the feeling resonated less. With every block, my vision blurred. The sky grew dark, the temperature dropped, my mother didn't know where I was, but none of it mattered. Nothing did.

After five miles, I had nothing left.

One more step, Harmony.

My head pounded inside my skull, keeping time with my heart breaking out of my chest.

Just keep going. Almost there.

Almost where?

It's almost over. One more step.

No. No more steps. I was sick of it.

One more step.

I wanted the voice in my head to stop. I wanted being a person to stop. I wanted everything to stop.

Don't fucking stop, Harmony.

Please. I was so tired. Please just let me stop.

One more step until it's over, Harmony. One more step.

Please stop.

It's never going to stop. There's always one more step. Stop waiting for it to stop. Stop kidding yourself that you're ever going to be rid of this. Stop believing that if you just push through you can reach the end of this, because it doesn't end. Because it's you. This is who you are. This is who you deserve to be. The only way this will stop is when you stop. And you're too much of a pussy to do even that. So take one more step, Harmony. Just one more. And then a million more.

Ok. One more step. One more. One more.

And that's when I slipped. The ground was slick with ice, and in crossing the street I put my foot down and it rushed out from under me. Before I knew what had happened, I was eating slush in the gutter. My forehead burned, and something dripped into my eyes. My legs splayed out in the street behind me. Headlights illuminated my face. I heard a screeching of tires.

I closed my eyes, almost choking with gratitude. Finally. Finally it would stop.

But it didn't. It didn't stop, because the car did. About a foot from my face, spraying an additional layer of icy mud into it.

Close, but no cigar.

The thought occurred to me out of nowhere, and I heard hysterical laughter that for some reason was coming from my mouth.

"Holy shit, kid. What the fuck?" A pair of work boots appeared in front of my face. Rory wore work boots like that, sometimes. But Rory was gone.

I couldn't stop laughing.

"Dude, oh man. Oh man are you okay? What the hell is wrong with you that you're lying in the gutter?"

What the hell is wrong with you?

He grabbed me under my arms and hoisted me to my feet as if I weighed no more than a sack of flour. My feet found the ground beneath them and I steadied myself, dimly aware that his hands were still gripping my arms, holding me up.

Someone else was holding you just like that.

I couldn't remember who.

"I slipped. I was- I was running." I managed to get out through my hiccuping remains of laughter.

The guy with the work boots, who looked maybe 40 and was wearing an orange construction vest, looked at me as if I were crazy. To be fair to him, that's probably how I would have looked at myself too.

"Kid, we gotta call like an ambulance- something. Your head's bleeding- that shit looks pretty deep. Fuck, kid." He finally released his hold on me, running his hands through his overgrown afro while he stepped back and looked at his car in disbelief. "I almost just ran you over. I barely even saw you till I was right on top of you. Don't you know how late it is?"

Shit.

My mother. For the first time, I noticed that the sky was in the last shades of gray before black, and the streetlights were on.

"Can I use your phone? I have to call my mom."

"Can you use my phone? Shit, kid. I coulda just killed you. Take the damn phone!"

I thanked him calmly and dialed, though it took me five tries to get the number right. I couldn't feel the screen beneath my fingertips, and even then I could barely even see it.

She didn't pick up, so I left a voicemail telling her I'd be home soon.

"Thank you. Sorry about that." A voice that wasn't mine left my lips, and a purple hand extended to place the cell back in his.

Looking at my arm, his eyes widened. "Look, kid, you sure you ight? Let me at least drive you home."

"No, I'll just run. I need the exercise. Thank you anyway, though."

I turned back to where I'd come, but I couldn't remember where that was anymore. The street swayed and morphed in front of me as though it was lined with funhouse mirrors. I put one foot in front of the other and pumped my arms, starting a slow jog. I could hear the guy from the car yelling behind me, but I ignored him. My head was really starting to hurt.

To this day I cannot tell you how, but somehow I did manage to get home that night, around 8:00. All the lights in the house were on when I let myself in, and I soon found out why. My mother and Rory were sitting at the kitchen table.

He spoke first, rising half out of his seat as I came in the door. "Harmony- your head. Jesus kid, that looks deep. Are you alright?"

"Harmony?" My mom stood up, her eyes wide. "Where the hell have you been?" Before I could answer, her jaw dropped as she took in my full appearance. "Oh my god! Are you ok?? What the fuck happened, Harmony? I was worried sick."

I opened my mouth to tell her that I had slipped, that I had been out running, that I had tried to call her, that I was sorry. Instead, only two words tumbled out.

"I'm fine."

"Like hell you are! Do you know how fucking late it is? Do you know that Rory has been driving around the neighborhood ALL NIGHT looking for you? Do you know that we thought you were lost, or kidnapped, or raped, or DEAD?! What the hell is wrong with you?"

What the hell is wrong with you?

Her screaming was only making my headache worse. I felt hungover, though I couldn't remember drinking.

"Court, let the kid catch her breath. She looks like she just about got run over." Rory stepped slightly between my mom and me.

"RUN OVER?! DOES GETTING RUN OVER LEAVE YOU WITH CUTS A QUARTER INCH DEEP ALL OVER YOUR BODY? DOES GETTING RUN OVER MAKE YOUR THERAPIST TELL

YOUR MOTHER THAT YOU NEED TO BE HOSPITALIZED?" She shoved him out of the way, screaming hysterically.

My head was pounding. *Okay, okay, I'm sorry.* I tried to say. *I don't know what's wrong with me but I promise I won't let it worry you anymore. Just please, please stop yelling at me.* But nothing came out.

"Do you know how fucking hard I work, Harmony, so that you can have the life that you have? Tell me what is so fucking wrong with it that you do this to yourself. I don't know what the fuck to do with you. Everything I try, everything I do, and still you insist on being miserable. Do you understand what you're doing to your body? Do you realize that you'll have those scars forever, that when people see your prom pictures and your wedding pictures they'll ask me just what I did that made you so fucking crazy? No one will ever find that attractive, Harmony. No one will ever think you're brave or sexy or whatever it is that you're trying to be. Because it is none of those things. It's *none* of them. It's ugly. And I did not raise my only daughter to be ugly."

The room spun. I wanted to answer her, but I just needed to sit down first. I just needed to-

Everything disappeared, and the world was black. For one brief instant, everything stopped.

Then her voice started again. I opened my eyes to find my face buried in Rory's jacket. His arms were wrapped tightly around me. I had fallen, passed out, and he'd caught me. It seemed like all I ever did was need people to hold me up.

"Courtney." I heard his voice say. "Stop it. She's heard enough. Just let her take a shower and go to bed."

I wasn't sure if I'd just imagined him saying the words, because my mother didn't seem to hear them. She grabbed my arm, her nails digging into and opening cuts, and spun me away from him.

"Listen to me, Harmony. Let's hope you're still able to do that much. You will pull yourself together and get better, do you fucking hear me? You're not stupid, you're not crazy, I don't know what the fuck is wrong with you Harmony but god help me you will figure it out. Here, in this house, not in any goddamn hospital. You are FINE. Pull your head out of your ass and realize that you are *fine.* I grew up with jack shit, Harmony, and I managed. I did it. So you bet your ass you should be able to too." Her eyes burned into mine, and in that irrational moment, I knew she believed everything she'd said. I knew that she hated me. Later, I would convince myself that she had just been driven to hysteria with worry, and that she hadn't meant any of what she'd said that night, but in that moment, I knew better. She had meant every word.

"Go to bed, Harmony." Rory's voice, the only thing that was clear through the din inside my head. I tried to run, but my legs seemed to have forgotten how to be legs. I tripped, stumbled, and stepped in the cat's water dish. I heard the utensil drawer open. My mother was still yelling.

I found the stairs, and set my focus on them. Just one more step until I was there.

Just one more step.

It will never stop.

What the hell is wrong with you?

Something bounced off the wall where my head had just been. Something metal, something sharp. I deciphered one sentence from the incessant screaming: "Do you wanna take these with you, Harmony?!"

I made it all the way up the stairs, down the hall, and into the bathroom before throwing up everything in my stomach, which wasn't much. The only thing I can remember thinking is: vodka burns just as much coming up as it does going down.

I must have passed out on the bathroom floor, because the next thing I knew, I was in bed. The next morning, I would decide that it had to have been Rory that had brought me there. That night, though, that long, neverending night, all I could think about was getting onto the roof.

The next morning, I didn't see my mother at all. Rory drove me to school, stopping at Dunkin on the way and ordering half the damn menu. "You eating that is non negotiable." He informed me, setting the bags in my lap.

"Thanks." I pulled out a slightly squashed ham and cheese croissant, which he knew was my favorite. It tasted like paint thinner and sawdust.

"So, you're moving back in?" My throat had never felt so dry.

He shrugged, changing lanes without a signal. "I missed the cat."

When he dropped me off, he told me to have a good day, and that he'd pick me up after school. I said ok, see you then. I wanted to tell him I loved him, but I don't know if it's because I actually did, or because I just wanted to hear him say it back. Either way, neither of us said anything else.

That day, Noah Andrade was suspended for punching a kid so hard in the face, three of his teeth were knocked out.

That afternoon, I met Dr. James for the first time.

And that night, Hannah's father died.

PART FIVE

How to Save a Life

Jacob Santanuno was the father of my best friend of nearly 10 years, Hannah. To say he and I were close would be an understatement, since she and I had met she hadn't had a mom and I hadn't had a dad- we used to joke that they'd run off together, but it was the type of joke that was never very funny.

When Hannah turned five, he taught her to ride a bike while I watched from the front steps everyday. That summer, when my birthday rolled around, Hannah was the one watching, and I was the one learning, but the teacher hadn't changed. He was the one who taught me to always *always* wear a seat belt, because the mummy from Indiana Jones got injured in a car crash, and that's why he looked like that, and we didn't wanna end up like that, did we? Mr. Santanuno insisted on meeting not only every boy that Hannah went on a date with, but every boy that ever went out with me, too. Rory was my mom's boyfriend, and he was a good guy, but he wasn't a parent. He wasn't my dad. Hannah's father was.

We idolized him, both of us. When he met his second wife, Shauna, Hannah and her siblings hated her right away. Lenny, her brother, was probably the most upfront about it, but as soon as he moved out, Hannah took the reigns. She bitched about Shauna to me incessantly, but in five years, she never said one thing to her father. She never wanted him to be anything but happy.

When we were 12, he was diagnosed with stage three pancreatic cancer. We didn't know what that meant- not really. It was serious, they told us a million times, but never did it occur to me that he would die. Looking back, I'm not sure if it even occurred to me that he was *mortal*.

Hannah attacked it like she did everything else- as a project. We spent hours in her room pouring over library books and websites and anything we could get our hands on. It was Hannah who found the experimental treatment center in California. It was Hannah who begged her father to move across the country for it. She left everything that she'd ever known, everything that she had ever been, for him.

And then he died.

The night it happened, we stayed on the phone for hours. We weren't even talking, most of the time, just staring at each other's cross continental darkness. I'd never heard her cry before, but that night made up for 10 years of dry eyes. I listened to her heart break. And I said nothing.

The funeral was the week before Christmas, and they flew back to have it here. I walked through the line, and hugged Shauna and Lenny and Hannah and their little sister Layla, but I couldn't look at him. I didn't want to see his eyes closed. I didn't want to be reminded that there was nothing but cotton behind his eyelids.

Hannah's step mom and siblings spent the week in a hotel, but Hannah stayed with us. My mom left us alone, and we spent every night watching movies and drinking the cheap beer that Rory conspicuously left where we could find it. She refused to climb up to the roof, so the night before she left, we sat on the back steps so she could smoke until the sun came up.

"I wish you could stay for Christmas." I said truthfully.

"Honey, me too. I didn't even realize I missed it here till I came back. I almost wish that we could move back, now that he's dead. But there's nothing here for me anymore." She wrapped her arms tightly around her legs. It must have been 30 degrees, but we both sat in hoodies and sweatpants.

"Does it feel the same? You know, as when your mom died."

She shrugged. "Nah. I was so little then. My mom- she may have given birth to me, but she didn't raise me. She was my mother, not my momma, you know? I wasn't even three when she had that accident. Lenny, though... I think he remembers. I think it feels the same for him."

I nodded. My father was gone, run off before I could walk, and I didn't remember him at all. I had never felt a hole in my life where I'd felt like a father should be. I'd never felt like one was missing. Until now.

"What now?" I asked. "What do you do now?" *What do I do now?*

"I keep going." She threw the butt of her cigarette onto the sidewalk and stubbed it out with her toe, then shook another one out of the pack she kept in her hoodie. "I cry, and I get drunk a couple times, and I leave flowers on his grave, and I keep going. What else can I do? He's the one that's dead, not me. I gotta learn how to live without this part of myself now. I can't just stop."

"Don't you ever wish you could stop, though? Don't you ever wish it would all just end?"

"Sure I do. That'd be easier, but it's not about easy. That's not how it works. That's not how this is supposed to end. If it was, then what would be the point?"

I picked at my cuticles, chapped and raw from the cold. Numb. "What if there is no point?"

"Then why are we here, Harm? If there isn't a point then what are we doing here? Doesn't this mean something? Didn't my dad *mean* something? Don't ask me what, cause I don't know, but I have to believe that he meant *something*. I have to believe that the pain and hurt I feel right now is for a reason. That I'm supposed to do something with it. Learn from it, change from it, *something*. You only get one life, Harmony. I don't know who the fuck would be stupid enough to just throw it away."

Hannah Santanuno. My best friend of ten years. We grew up together. Went to school together. Made all the same friends. We'd been raised by the same man. And yet something was wired in her that was disconnected in me. I don't know why, but somewhere along the road she had turned the right way when I'd turned the wrong one.

I didn't answer. I didn't want to tell her that she believed something that I didn't. I didn't want to say that I really didn't see a point, or a reason, or anything. Maybe it's cause I *was* stupid, but if I was her I *would* have thrown my life away in that moment, just as easily as she had tossed out her cigarette. Stubbing it out of existence on the concrete.

For some reason, I thought of Noah, and of what he had said to me a year before, on an otherwise irrelevant day in gym class. *There are other ways to feel, you know, Harmony.*

But I didn't know. He did, and Hannah did, and her father had. They had something that I just didn't. Some instilled will to be alive, to be anything, solely because they felt they needed to be.

We sat in silence for the rest of the night, Hannah and me, passing a bottle back and forth. She smoked a pack and a half of cigarettes, and the butts were still littered around the gutter months after she was gone. When Shauna came to pick her up to catch their seven am flight the next morning, I stood at the gate and hugged her goodbye.

"I love you." I said, glad that I could feel that much at least. "And I'm sorry about your dad. He was... he was really great."

She smiled. "I know." She said, and kissed my cheek. Her lips were warm on my icy skin, and her breath smelled like cherry lollipops, not a trace of the tobacco scent from the night before. She was already moving forward, I realized.

"Stay gold, Ponyboy." She raised a hand and climbed into the Uber. Her brilliantly red curls were fire in the early morning dawn, her cheeks were bright pink, her eyes were shining as she turned toward the road in front of her.

I stood on the curb until the car was out of sight, but she didn't turn back.

I never saw her again. Nothing gold can stay, afterall.

PART SIX

Just a Dream

Me: Have a good christmas.
Noah: awww thank you merry christmas to you too!

Things went back to normal soon enough. Every once in awhile, I touched the book of addresses and phone numbers that my mother had kept since I was five, thumbing through the pages until I found the Santanuo's number. House phone, and Jacob's cell. In 10 years, his number hadn't changed once.

One day, when my mom and Rory were out, I did actually dial. I was thinking that at least maybe I'd get his answering machine, and be able to hear his voice. The phone only rang twice, though, before a recorded message told me the number had been disconnected. I shouldn't have been surprised, but for some reason the sound of the dial tone was what put me over the edge. The last string holding me together snapped. Even now, even after everything else, I really do believe that day was the day there was no going back. That was the day I gave up.

I wanted to call Hannah, too, at least she would answer, but I couldn't. She had been right when she'd said that there was nothing here for her anymore. Whatever she and I had been, we weren't anymore. She'd meant what she said about moving forward, and she hadn't looked back. She kept going, and I stayed stuck.

My mom was just about done trying to figure out what to do with me and so was I. I went to see Dr. James once a week, and I really did like her. It wasn't even that she gave bad advice, it was more just that she told me things I already knew, and was already ignoring. One suggestion she made that did stick, however, was the notion that I should get a job, probably because it was something my mother had already been hinting at for awhile. When I pointed out that I didn't need money because I never went anywhere or did anything, she asked me what about my friends, and I was stuck. I'd told her about Alana and Gio and Jess and Maya, and had succeeded in making it sound like we were close. Obviously too well.

"Yeah, I mean, yeah I got friends. But we don't really like, go out."

"Ever?" She raised an eyebrow, scribbling away on her pad. I sighed. She noticed, and put the pencil down. "Listen Harmony. I'm not naive enough to think that you follow up on every suggestion I make. In fact, I can tell that most of them go right over your head. But how in god's name do you actually expect to start feeling better if you stay inside all day and do nothing but homework and sleep? You don't have to get a job, but you have got to do *something.*"

"Okay, okay. I'll get a job. Happy?"

She glanced at me before dropping her gaze back to her pad. "Are you?"

Long story short, I did end up getting a job. It was three days a week at this crappy little 24/7 diner a block down from the 7/11 on Main Street. Getting that job ended up defining the rest of my year, but I'm getting ahead of myself again. For now, I'll just tell you about the first direct consequence, a situation which brought someone who's been dormant in this story for a little while back onto center stage. I've already told you that I wish this story could be about Noah, but there were periods of time, a painfully significant amount, when our paths seldom crossed. He had his own shit, much of which I did not learn the extent of till later, and I had mine. The night I was nearly hit by a car, my mother's resulting freak out, and the death of Hannah's father, are things I dealt with on my own. Getting a job at Freddie's All Night Diner marks the next section of this story, one that he played a central role in. And it started when I met his brothers.

I'd been working at Freddie's three weeks, primarily the after school shifts from three to seven on weeknights, but one Friday two weeks into the new year a coworker asked to switch shifts, and it's not like I was doing anything. It was the late shift, seven to eleven, and it had been an uneventful night overall, the usual drunk teenagers flipping over tables and then storming out, when three guys walked in.

There was nothing special about them at first, just three light skin teens blazed out of their minds, shoveling down some food before going home to crash. The two tallest, with matching milk chocolate skin and tattoos peeking from under their t shirts, slid into a bench against the wall. The smallest one looked less than a year older than me, he wore a letterman jacket for the Rosemont Tigers, which was our football team, though I'd never seen him around. I took a deep breath, and picked up my pad. It was almost 10. I could deal with one more table of assholes before the night was up.

"Can I get you guys something to drink?" The two on the bench looked up in turn, smiling at me in amusement. The biggest one smirked and put his hand to his mouth, running his tongue across his lips. "You sure can."

I wasn't amused, and neither was the kid in the chair. "Fuck off, guys." He said, turning to roll his eyes at me apologetically. "Can I get a coke?"

I nodded, and looked back at the kids on the bench.

"Let me get a Coors, babe." The oldest one said. I raised an eyebrow- the kid definitely couldn't have been more than 20.

"You got ID?"

"What you mean do I got ID? You don't know who I am?" He was laughing, but his eyes were serious. It was the first familiar thing I noticed about his demeanor.

"When he asks for something, you get it for him." The other kid on the bench said. He put his hand under the table kinda casual, but his tone was warning.

"ID." I said again. I knew boys, and usually they were all talk. However, while I was sure I'd never seen this group around before, somehow I did feel like I knew them, and for some reason, the feeling had a bad connotation.

He held my gaze for a minute, then reached into his pocket and produced his license.

The shit looked fake for sure, but I wasn't paying enough attention to that. I was distracted by the name written across the bottom of the card.

Cameron L. Andrade.

"Satisfied?" Cameron asked roughly. I shouldn't have been, I should have made them leave right then and there, but instead I nodded.

"Fine. But I know the rest of y'all not 21 for sure. One Coors and two cokes." I swallowed and turned to walk away.

"Some burgers too, ight?" One of them called after me.

"Sure." I nodded, but I couldn't turn around. I couldn't turn around because I knew that if I did, I would see him in all three of them.

I tried to ignore it as I brought them their drinks. Who cared if they were Noah's brothers? Who cared if they were infamous throughout the school? What did it matter if they were drug dealers or gang bangers or if they'd spent time in juvie or whatever. They weren't him. They may have shared his DNA and his daddy but that didn't mean they were anything but a pain in the ass to me.

"Burgers gonna be a couple minutes." I said after the three of them had their drinks. "You guys want anything else right now?"

"How bout your number?" The one on the bench that wasn't Cameron asked, and Cameron snickered.

"That's not on the menu tonight, sorry." I tried to keep my voice even, and turned to walk away, but he grabbed my wrist.

"Don't walk away from me, bitch." I looked down at his hand, at least twice the size of mine, wrapped around my wrist. It wasn't painful, but any tighter and it would have been.

"Bet you think you're pretty smart, huh? Making me look like an idiot." His grip tightened, but I refused to grimace. His expression was angry, indignant. The kid sitting across the table was trying to act like he couldn't hear the conversation. It was the look on Cameron's face that really freaked me, though. He may not have been the one touching me, but he was the one that put uneasiness in me for the first time. His eyes were unhinged, wild. I realized that these boys were more than all talk.

"I don't think nothing. Now let go." I was talking to the kid holding my wrist, but my eyes were on Cameron. I felt like if I looked away from him for even a moment, it would be one moment too long.

He licked his lips and smiled at me. I'd never seen eyes like his before. Dark and bright, like an animals eyes. Dangerous.

He reached out a finger and traced it up my wrist, still held in his brother's grip. I tried to hide my shiver, but I couldn't. I couldn't understand how he could look calm and insane at the same time.

"Damn." He said softly, as the pad of his index finger slid over the first ridges of cuts. "You a crazy bitch, huh?" He locked eyes with me, and I felt my blood run cold. It was Noah's eyes that were staring back at me.

"Okay, enough." The voice from across the table broke me out of my fixation, and I yanked my gaze away.

The youngest brother looked more than just annoyed now, he looked pissed. "Leave her alone, guy." He looked at the kid who had asked for my number. "Let go of her, Joel." I had almost forgotten that he was still holding my wrist. He looked at the kid in the letterman jacket, then to Cameron, as if waiting for approval.

The oldest boy reached for his beer and tipped it back, finishing almost half the bottle before setting it back on the table. He looked across to the kid who had spoken, and his eyes were dangerous again. Warning. The kid held his gaze for what was in my opinion a daring amount of time, before finally shrugging and looking out the window. "Whatever." He said. "I'm just tryna get my food, man, and it's not like she can bring it over if y'all are gonna keep messing with her."

I waited. My fingers felt numb. Finally, Cameron looked at Joel and jerked his head slightly. My wrist was released, and I resisted the urge to yank it back as quickly as possible.

"You should watch what you say, kid." Cameron said softly. "No one likes a bitch with an attitude."

"I'll remember that." My throat was dry, and I walked away quickly. This time, my hands were shoved deep in my pockets.

My heart was hammering out of my chest, and I dug my phone out of my pocket, pulling up Noah's instagram. Pictures of him with Gio, Devante, Andy, one at homecoming last year with a girl I didn't recognize. And one picture, an old one, from middle school probably, with a boy a little taller than he was, the two of them making gang signs for the camera, probably without even really knowing what they meant. He was tagged as jareddrade847. I looked back at the table of guys near the door. The one sitting in the chair, the youngest one. He looked the same, but the other two weren't anywhere on his page. I searched Cameron and Joel in his followers, and they came up, but both accounts were private.

I closed my eyes briefly, and told myself again that it didn't matter. I told myself that he wasn't them. I heard his voice on the day we'd first met- the rage when he thought Jason had put his hands on me. And again on homecoming night- his tense jaw when I was catcalled, his eyes on my collarbone, making me wear his sweatshirt. Again I felt Joel's hand on my wrist, Cameron's eyes all over my body. No. Noah wasn't them. Noah would never. I knew that.

I got them their food and asked again if they wanted anything else. When they said no, I thought I was in the clear, I thought I had gotten through the worst of it. Needing some air, I went outside to the back alley where the employees smoked on their brakes.

Leaning against the brick side of the building, I closed my eyes. I remembered Noah's breath down my neck the night of homecoming. I remembered how the pad of his thumb felt against my lips. Guys could say whatever they wanted, they could look at me however, they could even touch me, and I didn't care. Even if they were his friends or his brothers. As long as they weren't him. I could feel my breathing start to calm, as it always did when I thought about him.

And that's when the night went from bad to worse.

I had been nervous to take my eyes off of Cameron for even a minute, but I had, and I'd been right about it being one minute too long.

Breath like smoke slid across my neck, and I didn't even have to smell the Coors and pot on it to know who it was. I opened my eyes and tried to jerk myself off of the wall, but it was too late. His hands clamped onto my wrists, the blunt between his fingers dangerously close to my skin.

"You keep running away before I can ask for what I want." He whispered. Jesus. It was Noah's voice, too. Any sense of calm I'd managed to work back into myself vanished instantly. "There's cameras." I tried to say it forcefully, but my throat felt like sandpaper. He laughed, and moved closer.

"They don't work, and you know it." One hand held my right wrist firmly against the wall, but the other slipped between my legs. "You should've known better than to mess with my brother like that." His face rubbed against mine, rough with stubble. "I hate it when dumb hoes try to act smart."

I opened my mouth again to speak, but this time I couldn't even find the words. "Not so brave now, are you?" His hand was moving farther up my thigh.

He wouldn't dare, I tried to tell myself. He wouldn't really do it.

Christ, Harmony, are you this stupid? Of course he would. You knew it the minute you looked at him. This isn't just any kid, there's something wrong with him. You knew it, and you had to run your big mouth anyway.

Stupid stupid stupid. I hated myself for taking my eyes off of him. I hated myself for not kicking them out in the beginning. I hated myself for looking him up, as if I'd expected to find something I didn't already know. I hated myself for not screaming.

He didn't stop, of course. He kept talking, too, taunting me, while he felt me all over. I closed my eyes tightly while a single tear slid down my cheek. I knew I'd see Noah's eyes if I opened mine.

After five minutes he let me go, satisfied apparently. "Maybe now you've learned your lesson." He said when he finally backed off. I didn't respond. After that one tear, my eyes were so dry they stung.

He flicked his blunt onto the ground and spit on it, extinguishing it's glowing embers. "Shouldn't you be getting back to work? I think we're ready for the check." He smirked at his own cleverness, and in a minute he was gone.

I tried to force more tears into my eyes, but they wouldn't come. I tried to feel something, anything, but my whole body was numb. There was nothing for me to do, so I just went back inside. I brought them the check, going through the motions of printing it out and putting it in the folder robotically, without thinking about what I was doing. The dining room seemed a mile long as I walked across it to their table.

Joel and Jared were both on their phones, oblivious, and neither looked up when I put it down. Only Cameron looked at me. He was smiling.

Finally, I found my voice.

"You know, I know your brother, Cameron. I know Noah." The other two looked up, but as far as I was concerned, they didn't exist. I forced myself to keep looking at him, to keep staring into his black eyes that were so horrifyingly familiar.

"Yeah?" He raised an eyebrow. "What the fuck do you know about my brother?"

Harmony, don't say it-

"I know he's missed about ten days of school since you guys have been around. I know on the days that he does show up, it's like he's not really there at all. I know that sometimes he can barely even open his eyes, they're so swollen. I know that he can't even wear a backpack anymore, because his ribs are so bruised that he can't handle anything brushing against them. I know that he hates when people call him by his last name, because as soon as people know he's related to you, they don't want to know anything else about him."

I said all of it looking right at him. I watched his eyes change, from amused to shocked to indignant to furious. It was the stupidest thing I've ever done in my life, and I knew it as soon as I said it, but I couldn't have taken it back, and I didn't want to.

"Have a goodnight." I said stiffly, then walked away as quickly as possible. I heard the door of the restaurant open and close, but I didn't look up to see if they had left. I'd already used up all the stupid courage I had in me.

"Hey." I jumped at the voice next to me. I don't know what I would have done if it had been Cameron.

But it wasn't. Jared Andrade stood in front of me. I looked him over, uneasy.

He held out a folded bill. "Take it."

I just shook my head. "Don't worry about it." He rolled his eyes, and shoved the cash into my apron.

"You know Cameron didn't leave you anything."

"Thanks." I said tightly and turned away. I was waiting for him to leave, but he didn't.

"He's gonna end up just like them, you know."

He didn't need to specify who he was talking about, I already knew. My throat felt like it was closing up when I shook my head and answered, "Noah could never be that cruel."

I was wiping down the bar, but I heard him sigh from beside me, and I felt bad. He hadn't been the one that did anything wrong. I glanced at him. He looked more like Noah than either of the others, but with lighter skin, coffee milk instead of caramel, and hazel eyes. His mannerisms were the same though, the way he bit his nails and tilted his head, smiling kind of sadly at me.

"You care about him, don't you?" He had lowered his voice. I bit my lip and looked down. What could I have said? His eyes may have been a different color than Noah's, but they could still read me just as well.

"Look you seem like a nice girl, so imma give this to you straight." Out of the corner of my eye I could see him looking at me, so I lifted my head. "There's a lot that you don't know about my brother."

His eyes were empathetic, but they were serious too. He tapped the counter and let out a breath. "I'll see you around."

Just like that, the three of them were gone.

It was almost 11, and the dining room was nearly empty. Only me and one other girl were working, but I told her I'd close up if she wanted to leave, and of course she did. No one wanted to hang around that shit hole for long.

I didn't want to think while I washed down the table and swept the floor, so I turned the radio on full volume, until I couldn't even hear the vacuum cleaner over it, let alone my thoughts. When I finally finished around 12 it was snowing, and the streets outside were still packed with cars beeping and drivers yelling at each other, but the only people on the sidewalks were the ones my mom told me to stay away from. Before I started on my way home, I pulled my phone out again, and opened Noah's instagram. That picture from homecoming last year… he looked so much younger. The girl I didn't recognize at all, although she was tagged as Madeline_Friar. I stared at her face, trying to place her, but I couldn't. Looking between them I could see an innocent joy that looked so foreign on him. Who was she? Did she know what had happened to him, between the time that picture had been taken, and now? Would I ever know?

Do you even want to find out?

I stopped under the streetlight in front of the 7/11, the December wind tearing through my thin jacket. Noah was standing in front of me, the grayish snowflakes pearl white as they landed on his skin. He held his shirt up to his neck, exposing his chest. My eyes found the tattoo on his ribs, the scars on his side.

"It's okay, Harmony." He said quietly, in Jared's voice. Joel's voice. Cameron's voice.

I reached my hand out, but my fingers touched only air. My breath caught in my throat, and I slumped against the streetlight.

He wasn't there. I had no idea where he was. I heard the city sounds around me, and I knew that somewhere he was mixed into them, but I'd never know exactly where. Jared had been right. I didn't know him at all.

"Jesus Christ." My mother shook her head, turning back to the sink to finish the dishes.

"What's up?"

She shook her head disapprovingly, motioning to the tv. "Those kids are from your school."

I turned to the small device she kept in the kitchen, and sure enough, there was my school. With caution tape around it.

I grabbed the remote and turned the volume up. My mother always kept it low, she said she just liked to glance up and see the weather report while she was making dinner.

A pretty young reporter who had probably graduated herself less than five years ago was standing on the sidewalk in front of the school. *"Trouble today at Rosemont Senior High School, when a fight broke out on school grounds, leaving several students injured and two juveniles arrested, along with several other participants who do not attend the high school. This being Saturday, school was not in session, but the majority of the witnesses and participants in the fight are of high school age and attend Rosemont. Causes of the incident are still unknown, although several witnesses mentioned ongoing tensions between existing gangs in the area. Three minors were transported to Jackson Pediatric Hospital with non life threatening injuries."*

"I'll tell you, I'm glad you're not involved in that shit." My mom said, wiping her hands on the back of her jeans. "Sometimes kids act like they don't even got mamas. I may not have raised you perfect, but I know I raised you better than that, and you always had Rory and Mr. Santanuno looking out for you too. You've always known better than to mess with people like that."

I nodded, but I couldn't speak. My blood felt like it had been returned to my veins after spending too long outside of them. Cold, and like it didn't belong to me anymore. I don't know how, but somehow I knew, I *knew* that Noah had been there. I knew that Cameron and Joel had probably been the reason. And I had a terrible feeling of certainty that he had gotten hurt.

"Harmony? You okay?" My mom asked with some concern. She laid her hand against my forehead. "You feel a little warm, honey."

"I um. I don't feel great." I replied honestly. I didn't feel good at all.

"Go to bed, ok? And keep the window closed. I know you like to have it open, god knows why, but the cold air is only gonna make you sick."

I nodded, and left the room.

I wanted to text him, but if I did and he didn't respond, I'd only feel worse. Instead, I texted Gio.

Were u there today?

He responded immediately. nah but a lot of people were.

I swallowed, and forced my fingers to type, just one word. Noah?

It seemed to take him hours to respond, and I could feel my anxiety building with every second. Finally, the dots that meant he was texting appeared. I held my breath.

idk. i think maybe. he's not answering his phone.

I closed my eyes. I told myself that it didn't mean anything. I told myself that even if it did, the news had said non life threatening injuries. I told myself so many things that soon I couldn't decipher one from the other.

You've always known better than to mess with people like that.

What had I told him the first day we'd met?

I've never known what's good for me.

———— ∝∞∝ ————

Gio didn't hear from him all weekend. Nobody did. Monday morning, I didn't want to go to school- I was sure that he wouldn't be there. I didn't want what I already knew to be confirmed.

But of course, I did go, and of course I looked for him everywhere. Of course he wasn't there.

Everybody was talking about the fight, I mean, it's not like anyone could ignore the blood stain in the parking lot. Whispered conversations and sideways glances in the hallways were the highlight of the day. Fights weren't uncommon at Rosemont, but for one to make the news was definitely something to talk about. Two kids had been arrested, seniors. Jason was one of them, he'd been held back again, but the other was a kid I didn't know. They hadn't been the only ones at fault and everyone knew it, but no one would drop any other names out loud, cause you never knew who was listening, and everybody knows that snitches get stitches. As for the boys at the hospital, I heard rumors, but it was clear that no one knew for sure. No one knew anything.

By the time school got out, I had heard his name more than a few times, but I still hadn't seen him once. He had been there, that much was pretty certain, but whether he had started it, ended it, or ended up in the hospital, no one seemed to know. I thought about what he'd said once, about people only knowing him by the things he'd done, or the things they thought he'd done. I didn't want to believe any of what I'd heard, I didn't want to think about him as Cam Andrade's kid brother, or as the kid who started fights, or as anything but Noah. As anything but my friend. I wanted to believe that I knew who he was. Honestly, I just wanted him to be okay, but as the day wore on, it became increasingly clear that he wasn't.

I walked to my bus on feet that were made of lead. The snow falling softly from the sky was ironically beautiful, crystal white and sparkling in the sunlight as it landed on the blood stained pavement. Boys were running around, picking up handfuls of snow and throwing it at each other. Snowstorms and gym class are the two things that can make teenage boys forget about acting cool, and turn into six year olds again. The girls squealed on the occasions that they were caught in the crossfire, they called the guys assholes and jerks, but they couldn't hide their bright eyes and pink cheeks. I watched as Jessica snuck up behind her boyfriend and jumped onto his back. I watched Gio scoop up a handful of the icy white substance and pour it down the back of Alana's coat. She shrieked, whipping around to slap him hard, while Andy and Devante laughed. Devante lugged an armful of the stuff in Gio's direction, only to be hit in the side of the face by a surprise attack of his own, thrown from a boy standing a ways away.

I thought I was dreaming when I heard Lexi scream, "Noah!"

I froze. As if in slow motion, I watched a boy run across the pavement. The flakes of snow clung to his hair just as I'd imagined they would have on Friday night. He was wearing the Adidas sweatpants along with his old red and white Jordans, and a black t shirt with a picture of Tupac on the front. No jacket, but if he was cold, he didn't show it. His lip was busted up pretty badly, and half his face was swollen and purple, but his eyes were still the brightest I'd ever seen them, and his smile made the imperfections on his skin irrelevant.

Noah.

I could have choked with relief, I hadn't let myself realize how truly certain I had been that something had happened to him until I saw that it hadn't.

Standing still, it was all I could do to keep breathing. The flood of emotions, the only ones I'd felt for weeks, sweeping through my body all at once was too much.

I watched as, still laughing, the boy bent to scoop snow from the ground. He formed it into a ball in his ungloved hands, scanning the mass of unsuspecting kids for his next target. Finally, he wound up to throw, and his aim was dead on, hitting a kid with a bleached high fade 20 feet away. They chased each other around the parking lot like little kids, ducking behind girls and teachers, slipping on the icy cement. At one point, he tripped and slid five feet on his ass, giving the other boy a chance to catch up to him. They tackled each other and rolled into the snowbank. I watched as two boys acted their age, harmlessly wrestling to no means, with no risk of getting hurt. The kid with bleached hair got up finally, brushing slush off his jeans before running off with a grin. I watched as the remaining boy sat up, holding a handful of snow to his broken face while he waited for his friends to congregate around him.

Noah.

I wanted to say it so bad. I wanted to go over to him, to hear his voice, to see his eyes and be reminded that black eyes could be warm not just cruel, to touch him like I'd wanted to on Friday night. But I couldn't.

The boy stood up, brushing off the seat of his sweatpants. He was talking to his friends, laughing and shaking his head so his overgrown curls fell into his face. I watched as his expression changed, from exuberant to amused to shocked to a hundred other different things in the span of just a few moments.

Noah.

I watched him grab his backpack and pull it onto his shoulders, slapping palms with the guys around him before starting his walk home with a couple of his boys.

Noah.

I watched him pick up a handful of snow and rub it into Gio's hair. I watched him grab the straps of his backpack and grin as he dodged his friend's retaliation attack.

Noah.

Then I turned, and walked away.

PART SEVEN

Breathe (2am)

The bus ride home was bittersweet. I texted him- i was worried about u, im glad you're ok- but I didn't expect a response. I hadn't had the courage to reach out to him when it counted, and seeing him had reminded me just how impossible the situation was. What did I know about Noah, really? What was it about him that made me want to know more? I was crazy if I thought that I could live like this- worrying for days because I was terrified that something had happened to him, when I had no way of knowing if he would do the same for me.

I was crazy if I thought I could go on living at all.

The bus dropped me off a block from my house, but the walk down my street seemed longer. I remembered walking with him along the same street in October, but for some reason, the memory seemed blurry. I remembered what he'd worn, the things he'd said, I remembered thinking we were friends, real friends. I remembered falling asleep in his sweatshirt. But how much of it had been real? Looking back, it felt like it had been just a dream, like the song said. As if I'd imagined everything. I'd felt like I knew him, but did I? When he smiled at me, held me, I felt the closest to okay that I'd felt in a long time. Was that who he was- a boy who threw snowballs and walked me home and always had my back when I least expected it? Or was he who everyone else said he was- a kid who started fights, who could never control his temper, who was walking down the same road as his father and his brothers?

Thinking about it all made my head hurt. I didn't know, I wanted to, I wanted to reach out to him, to close the distance that always seemed to be between us, but for some reason, I just couldn't. Going looking for answers would put me in a situation that I was afraid of. I cared about him more than I'd ever cared about anything, but if what people said was true, then I had fallen for someone who would never even look my way, and what did that make me? Pathetic, an idiot?

But who was I kidding? Wasn't I already those things anyway? Even if every rumor about him was true, even if he *would* turn into the monster that Cameron was, Noah was ten times the person that I would ever be. He was the one that always closed the distance, wasn't he? I just sat around and waited. Useless, like always.

By the time I got home, I was sure of two things. I was in love with Noah Andrade, but I would never love myself. Because how can you love something that doesn't exist?

I wasn't a person, I was a waste of space, a liability to everyone and everything in my life. I could look at Noah and see a million things. I could think about Hannah, and a thousand things would come to mind. I could remember her father, and the memory would last all day. My friends, my family- I was surrounded by people everyday who were full of happiness, ambition, confidence, life, and yet none of it resonated with me. A disconnected circuit, a broken mind, a wrong turn, I could use as many metaphors to describe it as I wanted, but nothing would change the ultimate truth. I wasn't meant to be me. Everything in my life worked, nothing was wrong with it. I was the only puzzle piece that didn't fit. My name might have been Harmony, but it was the farthest thing from what I was, and if I wasn't myself, then who was I?

Without remembering how I got there, I found myself standing in front of my bedroom window. Somehow, it seemed to be where I always ended up.

I opened the window without telling myself to. Climbed onto the sill. One foot on the railing. Hands on the roof. Hoisted myself over. No slipping this time. This time, nothing would be on accident.

Pulling myself to my feet should have been difficult, but it wasn't. I wish I could say something poetic, like I felt as though I were moving outside of time, in a sequence of events that only I existed in. But in reality, nothing is ever poetic. Blood isn't a particularly beautiful color when it's spilling from your wrists. Tears aren't especially salty when you don't know why you're crying them. And life isn't suddenly worth living when you're about to end it.

The toes of my sneakers were on the edge of the roof, the rubber tips edging over the shingles. I looked down, and there was my body on the sidewalk below me, the limbs twisted in unnatural directions, the hair matted with blood, the face bruised. It was my body, but I was no longer in it. Where whatever was left of me had gone I didn't know, but it wasn't here, it wasn't in this life, and that was enough. That was all I needed.

I breathed deeply, wondering how many breaths I had left. As I sucked the winter air into my lungs, I thought about cellular respiration. The oxygen from the atmosphere was being broken down in my body to give me the ATP I needed to function. Funny how easily I could absorb the energy to live, but not the will to. I looked at my hands, and hated them, with their torn cuticles and chipping nail polish and awkward fingers. I hated my arms, and their layers upon layers of scar tissue and pathetic concealer cover-up. I hated my legs, which were wide in all the wrong places, and too long and too short at the same time. I hated my entire body, from my hips to my stomach to my breasts to my hair to my face. My stupid, pathetic face. I hated the thing inside of me that had no right to call itself Harmony. All I felt was hate.

I was ready.

Closing my eyes, I tilted toward the ground. I could feel myself start to lose my balance, and resisted the urge to swing my arms to regain it.

One more step, Harmony.

Just one more step.

I lifted my foot to step off

and felt my phone vibrate in my back pocket.

My eyes flew open. Seeing the ground leering up at me, instinct took over. I flailed my arms, jerking my body backwards just in time, so I landed hard on my ass on the roof. My hands stung as they embedded themselves into the shingling.

It took me almost a full minute to realize what had happened.

It took me almost a full minute to realize I was still alive.

Why was I still alive?

Your phone, dipshit.

I dug it out from where it was digging painfully into my tailbone. One message.

Noah: yea im ight. shit was wack. thx fa checkin in tho appreciate it. u straight?

No. No you are not, Harmony.

I reminded myself to breathe because I'd seemed to have forgotten how. My eyes stung like hell, but this time no one was smoking.

When I had myself together again, I slowly typed out a reply.

Yea, im good. Make sure u taking care of yourself, Superman.

I'm good.

I'm alive.

I should not be alive.

On the street below me, my mom's car pulled up.

"Harmony?"

I couldn't hide my cringe upon hearing my name. It was something I had been sure I'd never have to hear again.

"Coming, Momma."

I swung my leg over the side of the roof, feeling it land solidly on the railing beneath it.

That's that.

I don't believe that Noah's text saved my life for a reason. I don't believe that I was meant to live those extra five months for some purpose or greater good. It was a coincidence. A coincidence that happened to have drastic consequences, but a coincidence nonetheless. Fate didn't have plans for me or anything like that. I should have died that day, but I didn't. Simple as that. I stuck it out for another 143 days. No more, no less.

Amazing all that can happen in one three digit number.

PART EIGHT

Demons

"Noah Andrade."

"Sure, I know him. I mean, we're friends."

Mrs. Couto raised an eyebrow at me. "Do you have any idea where Mr. Andrade was on the night of April 31st of this year?"

Yes.

"No ma'am."

She put down the folder she was holding and leaned across the desk between us. I don't know if it's a rule for all guidance counselors to have haircuts at least 10 years out of date, but if it is, Mrs. Couto is no exception.

"Harmony, this is a very serious issue. Cameron and Joel Andrade have not been seen or heard from since the night in question. It is assumed, with good reason, that they may have been the main perpetrators of the incident."

I nodded. So far, I was safe. Everyone knew about Joel and Cam ditching town. But my palms were sweaty. I knew what she was going to say next.

"The victim reported three people at the scene of the crime, Harmony." Her voice was even, direct. I could feel her looking at me, and I reminded myself to look back. Eye contact was important.

Especially when you were lying.

"There aren't many potential witnesses, but there are even fewer potential suspects. All the police need is one person to say one name, and then this whole thing can be over and done with." Her eyes were like reheated coffee. Lukewarm, and bitter. "I'm asking you again, Harmony. Do you have any idea where Noah was that night?"

I know exactly where he was. Because I was there too.

I looked directly at her, and my voice was even when I answered. "I'm sorry. I don't."

She let me leave. On my way out, I passed Jason in the hall. He stared me down through two bruised and swollen black eyes.

Shit.

Three months earlier

Despite my personally falling apart Sophomore year, in order to save face, my social life had to remain at least somewhat intact. That meant continuing to hang out with Jess and Taylor and their boyfriends, and, on occasion, relenting to one of the numerous party invitations Alana threw my way.

Partying with Alana and the PINK girls, as I'd come to call them, had been weird at first, but I adapted pretty quickly. The first struggle had been figuring out what I was supposed to wear- tube tops and mini skirts just made me look like a whore, though girls like Lexi could pull them off fine. On the other hand, there were girls like Alana, who could look like movie stars in their perfect makeup, messy buns, oversized hoodies, and sweatpants. I finally settled on the jeans and crop top look, and no one ever said anything about it one way or another, so I figured I was in the clear.

Then there was Jared Andrade, who showed at a few of the parties, although he was almost a year ahead of us. He was always polite, and never let on that we had met before in front of anyone else. I think we both knew it was for the best.

Finally, there was the elephant in the room. Having a social life meant, to an extent, having a boyfriend. Alana and Gio were getting pretty serious, and Lexi had started clinging on to Jaideson more and more. The question of when I was going to get myself a guy was raised more than once, to the point where I was having trouble coming up with an answer. Alana, as always, took it upon herself to solve that problem for me. One night, when maybe 15 people were chilling at her house, she slyly snuck a glance at me, then, with as little subtlety as possible, dared Devante to kiss the prettiest girl in the room.

I don't know if she had talked to him beforehand, but he immediately looked at me. He wasn't the only one. Across the dimly lit basement, Noah was staring at me too. He had one of the girls straddling his lap, and his hands were on her ass, but he'd clearly been listening. The kiss with Devante, along with the standard "oooohs" that followed, barely registered with me. I was too busy trying to figure out just what exactly Noah's eyes were telling me.

I ran into him later, when I was upstairs getting a drink. Alana drank rum with diet coke and Malibus, and while neither was really my thing, I knew there was no way I'd be getting through the whole night sober, not the way that things were going so far.

"I'll get it." Noah took the can out of my hand.

"Thanks." He nodded, chewing on his lip while he reached for a plastic cup. I leaned back against the counter, closing my eyes. The kitchen was bright compared to the basement, and my head hurt.

"He likes you, you know."

I opened my eyes, but he wasn't looking at me. He was focused on making the drink.

"Yeah." I shrugged. "I know."

He finished pouring the coke and crushed the can in his fist. "Do you like him?" His voice was tight.

"I don't know." I was being careful. Devante and Noah were friends. If I said I didn't like him, Noah might be pissed. Then again, knowing him, he'd probably find a way to be pissed either way. Also, Devante was cute, and he'd always been sweet to me, though I'd never really thought about it before.

"Well." Noah finished mixing the drink and handed it to me. Mostly soda, I noticed. He knew I was walking home. "I don't think you should do anything until you know."

I accepted the cup, but didn't take a sip. "When did you get so smart?" I asked him teasingly. He smiled slightly, and his hand reached out to brush my hair back. His fingers lingered on the back of my neck, right where my pulse was. I was sure he could feel it speeding up.

I should have told him to move, but I didn't want to. I knew he was looking at me, but I closed my eyes. Looking back at him was too complicated, it would only remind me of everything else. I just wanted to stand still in that moment forever, feeling the warmth of his skin against mine.

"Noah?" He dropped his hand, and I opened my eyes.

The girl who he'd been with earlier was standing in the kitchen, looking at us. Looking at him rather, she didn't even spare me a glance.

"I was looking for you. Alana said it would be okay if we went upstairs..." She trailed off, but she may as well have just come out and said it.

"Um." He cleared his throat, blinking rapidly. "Yeah, fine. Whatever." I looked between them, trying to see the attraction. She was kind of forgettably pretty- white, with thin hair, heavy makeup and a flat stomach. Definitely not a knockout, like Jess or Alana. The type of girl whose name you wouldn't remember the next day. Then again, I was the type of girl whose name you didn't even bother to learn.

She smiled seductively and grabbed his hand. The hand that had just been on my throat.

"I'll see you later, Harmony." His voice was flat, and his eyes, so bright just a moment before, were as dim as the basement.

"Sure." I nodded, but I knew I wouldn't be seeing him later at all.

I watched them leave the room and go upstairs, before turning around to realize I wasn't alone.

Jared stood next to the fridge, a half finished beer can in his hand. He rubbed a hand over his waves before dropping it into his pocket. His posture was relaxed, but his expression was anything but.

"He's like a clone, you know." he said after a moment.

I didn't answer, but I didn't leave either. No matter how comfortable I was becoming at these parties, there were still only a few people I was relaxed enough to let my guard down around. With Noah upstairs, and Alana and Gio off who knows where, I knew I was safest in the kitchen with Jared, where it was brightly lit, and there was nothing between me and the front door. The basement held too many shadows, too many dark corners, too many unfamiliar faces and groping hands.

So I stayed, but didn't speak, instead turning to the sink, which was full of dishes. I plunged my hands into the sudsy water, watching the scars on my wrists disappear inch by inch. The soap stung my skin, but I ignored it. I was anxious, and washing dishes gave my mind something to do. Like his brother, Jared filled the silence without prompting.

"He won't remember." He said. His voice moved to me across the kitchen, running over my skin until it reached my fingertips. I shivered, and he paused. I could feel his eyes on me, to see if I was listening. Composing myself, I swallowed, and pulled a plate out of the water to hold it under the faucet. Satisfied, Jared continued.

"He'd be too young. He doesn't see it. Not the way that I do."

I couldn't help it; my curiosity won out, and I glanced at him to show my confusion.

"When I was his age, and Joel was mine, Cam just a little older, this was how it happened. A different girl, every party, every week. They'd disappear upstairs, for an hour, two maybe. They thought they were scoring big- smoking what they wanted, drinking what they wanted, fucking whoever they wanted." I winced at the sudden sour turn of his voice. My knuckles were white around the plate in my hand.

"Watching Noah, it's like watching a rerun. It's the same thing, all over again. It's just the way that they are. Like they're genetically programmed." His voice faltered, lost its edge, and I had to strain to hear his next words. "Our dad's like that, too."

"But you're not." I said suddenly. I lifted another plate out of the water, wiped it dry, and turned to put it in the cupboard, but Jared was already there. I handed him the plate without thanking him, and turned back to the sink.

"I got lucky. Football, my grades... me and my girl have been together since seventh grade. I saw what my brothers turned into, hell, I saw what everyone in this town turns into. I promised myself, and my momma, that would never be me."

"Oh okay, so you're just better than him? Is that it? Out of the four of you, or like you said, out of the whole school, only one kid gets to turn out okay? The rest of us are all fucked, right?" I was surprised to find myself yelling at him; I hadn't meant to. I knew on some level he was right, and that I was jumping to conclusions, but it felt so good to be angry. It felt so good to *be* something.

"You know that's not what I meant." He said quietly. I looked at him, and his eyes made the anger inside of me disintegrate. He was so much like Noah, but he couldn't see it.

"I see the way you look at him, you know." I opened my mouth to rebuke him, but what could I have said? There, in the merciless light of the kitchen, under the thrall of his eyes, there was nowhere left to hide, and we both knew it.

"Every girl thinks they're going to be the one to make the bad guy turn good." He continued softly. "Every girl thinks they can be the one to help him change. And every time, all they do is get themselves hurt."

"Well one of them has to be right." I said without thinking. "I mean one of them has to be the one to help. Right?"

"Or he's just a bad kid." Jared said. "Some people you just can't help, kid. That's just the way it is."

He touched my shoulder, and went to leave the room, but my voice caught him.

"You told me there's a lot I don't know about him." I said. He turned around. "Well, there's a lot that you don't know, too."

Jared sighed. His left hand lingered on the basement doorknob, but his right reached up to the back of his neck. He stared across the room, past me, to the stairs leading to the second floor. I could hear noises from up there, and I know he could too.

"There's a lot I don't want to find out." He said after a while. His eyes were squinted almost shut, as if the light was hurting them. "I hope I'm wrong about him. Really. The kid's my brother... you think I don't love him too?"

I was about to tell him that we hadn't been talking about love, but I guess maybe we had. He had already left, anyway.

I stayed in the kitchen for the rest of the night, which albeit wasn't very long. People started leaving around 12, but when Devante offered to walk me home, I told him I would just stay the night. He was visibly disappointed, but I let him kiss me goodnight to soften the blow. A week later I *would* let him walk me home, and the week after that, he'd walk me to my room.

That night, though, we just stood on Alana's steps. He cupped my face when he leaned in, but my pulse didn't quicken. I kissed him back, but I didn't close my eyes.

"Everybody else left besides you and Lexi, so we're just gonna crash in the basement, okay?" I turned to see Alana standing behind me. The dusty porch light looked brilliant in a halo around her glossy hair. "Do you need to call your mom?"

"I already talked to her." Which was true.

The other girls poured themselves more drinks before going downstairs, but I decided I was done for the night. The basement was still trashed, but Alana pushed aside an array of red solo cups and forgotten panties to make room on the floor for a couple blankets. Where her parents were I have no idea, but I know that mine wouldn't have put up with that shit.

"You okay, Harm?" I turned to see Alana looking at me, and it only took me a few seconds to come up with a pursed lip smile. She beamed back and leaned in swiftly to kiss my cheek. For a moment after, my smile was genuine. She was a good friend to me, Alana, and if you're reading this now then I hope that things turned out well for her, I sincerely do. I hope that things turned out well for all of them.

They kept talking amongst themselves for awhile, and my mind drifted back to the events of the night. Jared's voice in the kitchen, as dusty as the particles illuminated by the dull light, muddling the sharpness of his words. Noah's voice before his, his pained expression and calloused hands. Then before that, Devante's eyes in the muted light of the basement as he leaned into me. So many boys, my whole life. Their faces drifted in and out of my mind- Devante, Gio, Jason. The boys in the car the night of homecoming. Jared, Noah, Joel. Cameron. Weren't they all Cameron?

"Harmony?" Alana nudged my shoulder as she reached across to grab her drink. "What's goin on in your head, girl?"

Oh, nothing. Just that I can't even be alone at this party because I know what will happen if I am, because it's happened before. It feels like it's always happening. Like that's all people will ever see me as. The only person, the only boy who has ever looked at me like I was more than something to feel up... he might end up being the worst of all of them. And even if he's not, he'll never love me. He's never loved anyone. I don't even know if he's ever had a real girlfriend. He doesn't do things like that- going to dances with girls, walking them home, making them feel special...

Except that he does.

Great, now you're getting off topic even in your head. You think boys are the only ones with one track minds?

"Harm?"

I looked up. She looked worried. I wanted to say something to reassure her, but at the same time I didn't wanna be dishonest. I couldn't have lied, anyway. I was a terrible liar when I was drunk. There were too many truths, and never enough lies to hide them all. So I tried to search through my overwhelming mirage of truths, in order to find one that would be acceptable to tell her.

Then I realized that I did, in fact, have something I wanted to ask her.

"Who's Madison Friar?" I asked.

Alana's face fell. "What?" She asked quietly, although I knew she had heard me.

"Maddie Friar. Shit, that's a name I haven't heard in a long time." After a long pause, Lexi's voice echoed in false casualness. I looked up. She was looking at me from across the room. Normally she ignored me if she could help it, she didn't dislike me anymore, I didn't think at least, but she would never be as warm as Alana. It looked like I had finally said the one thing that would drag her out of her phone. "She was Noah's girlfriend, freshmen year."

"Oh." I said. "I, um. I don't remember her." I could picture her face from Noah's instagram; pale heart shaped, with bright green eyes and thick dark hair.

"You wouldn't." Lexi said. Alana glanced at her, but she kept her gaze focused on me. "She was a year younger. An eighth grader, still at Massasoit."

"What happened?" I asked. Something about the way they were looking at each other had put a bad feeling in the pit of my stomach.

Lexi pursed her lips like she had tasted something bad, but her expression didn't budge.

"She got pregnant."

Oh.

Oh.

"Lexi." Alana's voice was sharp, but Lex kept her eyes on me. I could sense her looking me over, so I forced my expression to stay neutral.

"And that's why they broke up?" I phrased it like a statement.

"Lexi." Alana said again, spinning around to fix her with a warning look, but Lexi just brushed her off.

"No." She leaned forward. "It wasn't his." Alana sighed.

I swallowed. "*That's* why they broke up."

But again, Lex shook her head.

I looked between them, trying to decipher whatever anxious tension was clouding the air. This was already worse than I had imagined it could have been, but I could tell that there was something more. Something they weren't telling me.

"What?" I looked at Alana. "Whose was it?"

She turned to me slowly, as if doing so were painful. Her expression was torn; ripped in two so I could see her heart. Could see how broken it was. Her lips were parted slightly, and I could see the unspoken name resting on her tongue. With a horrifying sense of clarity, I realized I knew whose it was. That I had, perhaps, always known, from the second he pinned my wrist against the wall, and slid his other hand between my thighs.

Don't walk away from me, bitch.

"No." I whispered in disbelief, even as I heard my own thoughts echoing around my head.

Alana's face crumpled, and she looked back at Lexi. "You couldn't have just left it alone, huh? You had to start saying something you knew, you fucking *knew* you couldn't take back."

"Jesus, Lana, who the fuck do you think she's gonna tell, huh? Those prissy little student council girls she hangs around with? Give me a break. She asked, I wasn't gonna lie. She would've put it together eventually anyway."

Alana shook her head, her eyes glassy, but I realized that Lexi was right. The rest of the pieces were compiling in my mind faster than I could comprehend them, even before Lexi turned to me and finished the story. Noah's change in disposition after freshman year, all those missed days of school, the bruises, the unspoken conversations in the hallway. My head was spinning, but I forced myself to register her next words.

"Noah was livid. He went after them, stupidly. He wasn't thinking. That kid can take anyone in a fight, unless it's one of his brothers. They almost killed him. You remember that day, freshmen year, when he came back after being out for like a week, all fucked up? They put him in the fucking hospital. Cam told him that he was lucky they didn't do him even worse, and that from then on he should know better than to get in his way, cause he was gonna do whatever the fuck he wanted with whoever the fuck he wanted, didn't matter that he had six years on her, and if Noah went to the police or anyone about it, he'd do him *and* Maddie even worse than he already had. So Noah didn't know what to do. He couldn't go home, 'cause he never knew when Cam or Joel would swing by his momma's place, and he couldn't go to Maddie's, 'cause her parents still thought he was the one who'd fucked her up. He tried everything, I mean everything, to get to her, but she was too scared."

"She was scared he'd turn into Cameron, too." I finished for her quietly.

Lexi nodded. "He couldn't do nothing to get her back. I think that's what screwed him up the most, honestly. That look on her face. The way she flinched when he tried to touch her. But," here she stopped, and let out a dry laugh that was anything but humorous. "She still had a problem, and Noah felt more responsible than ever to take care of it. Biggest goddamn irony in the world, but he had to go to Cam and Joel for the money. He didn't have another option, hear? Cameron said they'd let him in on a couple of deals if he promised to keep staying quiet about the whole thing. So he got her the money, had to send it anonymously though, she didn't want anything to do with him at that point. She moved away the next month, and presumably got rid of it on her own." Again she paused, and wet her lips. She shook her head regretfully, her curls falling across her face.

"It's been over a year," Alana, who had been quiet, cut in. Her voice was like shattered glass. "It's been over a year, and Noah hasn't heard anything from her. He doesn't even know if she ended up getting the procedure, or anything."

My throat was dry, and I felt sick. "How do you guys know all this?" I asked in a voice that wasn't mine.

Alana's jaw set. "Because last year, Noah spent three months sleeping on the couch you're sitting on."

I closed my eyes, and could see him in my mind, almost too clearly. Could see him lying on the couch in the basement all alone, in the wintertime when the heat busted out, staring at the ceiling all night, wondering how the fuck he was gonna get up the next morning. The worst part was, I could see myself doing the exact same thing. How many times had we been awake together at 3am, just staring at nothing, and not known it?

"Everybody knows about Maddie getting knocked up last year, and Noah hustling drug money to get her an abortion. Everyone knows about how she left." Lexi said. She fixed her blue gray eyes on mine. "But me, Gio, Lana, and Jared are the only ones who know who that baby's daddy really was."

"And you." Alana said quickly. She moved onto the couch to sit next to me and leaned in earnestly. "But you won't tell anyone, Harmony. You won't." Her voice was pleading.

I swallowed, and realized that something needed to be said. "No." I said in the same foreign voice. I took Alana's hand and squeezed it. "No, of course not." She smiled slightly in exhausted relief.

"So he never went to the police." I looked back at Lexi.

She shook her head. "No, but they got busted the next month for some shit anyway. It was perfect, Noah got out of the gang shit and went back home. He got a whole ten months of peace."

"And then they got out." I said.

"And then they got out." She confirmed dimly. "Cam thought Noah had gone to the cops after all, and was the reason he and Joel got locked up. They caught up to him after school- two against one, he didn't have a chance. That time they really would have killed him, if Jared hadn't been there. That pissed them off, but they found a way to do Noah even dirtier than they could've with their fists. They got him back in the gang, doing the same shit as before, but even worse. Tried to get him initiated, you know, so he could start pulling even bigger shit for them. But Jared was in the way, getting in Noah's head, tryna talk him out of it. So they set him up. Part of initiation is you gotta kill somebody, you know, in another gang. That day, at the school, the day of the fight, it was supposed to be Noah's day. Only what Cam didn't tell him was that the kid he was supposed to take out knew about the whole thing, in fact he was supposed to be taking care of Noah, too. The meeting place was the high school, and Cam sent Noah there knowing he'd either kill or be killed- either way, he'd learn his lesson good. Only shit didn't go as planned."

"It was Jaideson who leaked the set up." Alana cut in. "He told Gio, who told Jared, who wasn't gonna let it happen- no way. So when Noah and the other kid showed up, a ton of other people were there too, Jared's friends. They tried to break up the fight, but then the bloods showed up and all hell broke loose. Noah managed to get out before Cam and Joel showed up, but..." She trailed off, biting her lip.

"But it was too late. Jared saved Noah's life, but he was already in too deep. When you start dealing like that, making easy money that way... it becomes like an addiction. You get hooked without even trying the drug itself." Lexi paused to look at me, and I nodded. Addiction was something I could understand, and I suddenly remembered a time when I realized Noah could, too.

"So he didn't get initiated. He's not in the gang." I said slowly. It should have been good news- it should have been what I wanted to hear, but I knew there was more. There was always more. A million steps.

"No, he's not. But he's still selling for them. He's still pulling jobs, in and out of school, all over. Why the hell do you think he hangs out with that Jason creep? Only no one's making him do it anymore. Sure Cam and Joel still beat on him, but they're not holding anything over his head anymore, see? They got what they really wanted." Alana paused, like the next sentence was too difficult to say, but I already knew what it was.

"They got him to be like them. Maddie was right, after all" I said. *Like they're genetically programmed.* So Jared was right. He was beyond saving. Just like me.

I looked across at Lexi, though not for confirmation; I knew I was right. "You didn't have to tell me this. You coulda left it alone, like Alana said."

She shrugged. "Noah doesn't talk to anyone though. Not anymore. None of us know what's going on in his head- not Jared, not Gio, nobody. Alana hates talking about it 'cause she's still got too much love for who he used to be. She hates being reminded about what he's turning into. But he trusts you, I don't know why. So I don't know. I guess I figured someone should know who didn't know him before. So maybe there'll be at least one person who can give a shit about who he is now."

I didn't know what to say to that. There didn't seem to be anything *to* say. I had a million things to think about, but my mind was blank. I just kept seeing him lying on the couch. I kept trying to imagine what he could have possibly been thinking about.

Later, I left them to go upstairs to use the bathroom. Looking at myself in the mirror, I could tell I was a mess. My makeup was smudged, my shirt sticky with something that had spilled on the couch, so I pulled it off over my head. I felt somewhat better after splashing cold water on my face, but I knew I was still a long way off from ever feeling really okay. I was such a mess; my body, my face, my mind. I stared at my arms, at the torn skin that stretched from wrist to shoulder. Stretch marks were visible at the edges of my bra. My stomach sagged, but my ribs poked out. My skin wasn't dark enough to be tan, but not pale enough to be translucent. All it was was ugly. God, I was so fucking ugly.

I knew I should have been realizing how much worse my life could have been, and feeling grateful and relieved that I didn't have to live through the unimaginable horrors that Noah had. First his brother rapes his girlfriend, then tries to kill him. Twice. Jesus.

Jesus Jesus Jesus.

Instead, all I felt was shame. What had I ever done to deserve the life that I had, and what could Noah have possibly done to deserve his? He was just a kid, still a baby in the retrospect of life, and he had already dealt with more shit than I would probably ever have to. Yet I was the one with the audacity to hate my life; myself.

Looking back up at the mirror, I felt an urge to hurt myself stronger than I ever had before. I wanted to scream at my reflection, to admonish it with profanities until it was permanently scarred. Until boys no longer looked at me like they wanted to know what was under my clothes. Until the ugliness under my skin shown through on top of it.

There's a Greek myth, about a servant to Athena who is raped by Poseidon, then turned into a monster so hideous that any human who ever laid eyes on her again would be immediately turned to stone. That's what I wanted. I wanted to turn myself into Medusa, so the whole world could finally see me for the monster I truly was, and then someone would come and cut my head off, and the whole thing would be over with. Goodbye, the end, happily never after.

I let out a dry little laugh, and raked my nails across my cheek- harder than I'd meant to. Small drops of blood like needle points landed in the basin of the sink in a way that in any other circumstances could have been considered pretty.

Leaning against the sink watching the rain of my own blood, I remembered something my mother had told me when I was little, about 90% of people looking through other people's medicine cabinets. Just for the hell of it, I opened the cabinet under the sink. Bandaids, q-tips, vaseline, tampons. And pills. Bottles and bottles of pills. I didn't know what any of them were, really, but a combination of most of them was sure to do something.

What do you have to lose?

My hand had closed around the first bottle when I heard a door open in the hallway.

"Shit." I closed the door as quietly as I could. Whoever it was was walking quietly, as if afraid to wake someone up. I considered waiting in the bathroom for whoever it was to leave, but their footsteps were coming closer to the bathroom. I stood up and spun around just as Noah walked into the room.

"Harm..." He stopped once he saw me, but didn't start. His hair was tousled in front of his eyes, which were only half awake. Without thinking, I let my eyes roam down his bare chest. He was wearing nothing but sweatpants, which hung low on his hips so his v line was exposed. I felt my cheeks heat up, and looked back up at his face. He met my eyes quickly, and I realized that he had been looking me over too. I suddenly remembered how exposed I was, and immediately raised my arms over my chest, even as he was looking away.

"I didn't know you were still here." He said quietly, still looking at the wall just to the left of my head. My cheeks were still pink and it looked like his were too, although I couldn't be sure in the dim lighting. There was really no reason to be embarrassed; we may as well have been in bathing suits, and it wasn't like he was a stranger. Still, standing unclothed, even partly so, in a house that wasn't mine, looking at a boy less than five feet away from me, in the dark no less, made me feel more vulnerable than I could remember feeling in a long time.

"I didn't know you were still here, either." I said once I had remembered how to use my voice.

He seemed to wait a longer than average amount of time before shrugging. "I fell asleep."

I couldn't help it, I scoffed a bit at that. "She was that bad, huh?"

"Something like that."

"I didn't recognize her." I said then. I desperately wanted to change the subject, but wasn't sure how.

He shrugged, and walked farther into the room until he could sit on the edge of the tub. "She's a junior, I think. Arianna something." He looked worn out. After a moment's hesitation, I sat next to him on the tub. I could see scratch marks across his back, and a hickey on his shoulder.

"So." He said after a pause. "You and Vante, huh?"

I shrugged. "I told you. I don't know how I feel. I haven't really thought about it."

"That's what I figured you'd say." He nodded, then glanced sideways at me. "Are you-" He cut himself off and shook his head, but I knew immediately what he had been asking.

"Noah, look at me. I mean Jesus, what do you think?" I gestured to my torso, momentarily forgetting my bare skin.

He allowed his eyes to glance briefly at my collar bone, before turning away again. "I think that I don't know." Was his answer.

"Well yeah." I said, suddenly feeling spiteful. "I am." The most sexual encounter I had ever had had been with Cameron, but Noah was just about the last person I was going to confide *that* to, especially after what I'd just learned about him.

"Well, he's not, you know." He responded. I said nothing, implying that I had both assumed as much and didn't care. "I'm just saying, be careful." HIs voice was subdued, yet underlyingly dangerous.

He's just as afraid of it as you are. In a different way, maybe, but he was, I realized. He knew just how badly it could go wrong.

"Devante wouldn't hurt me. He's not... he's not other people."

Noah glanced over at me quickly, careful to keep his eyes on my face, when suddenly they widened. "Harmony. Jesus. Your face." His expression hardened from surprise to fury. "Did someone touch you?"

He closed the space between us before I knew he was even moving, and without warning his hand was suddenly on my torn cheek. Before I might have been startled, even scared he was moving in on me, but now I knew the reason behind his concern. The first day we'd met... the fury in his eyes when he thought Jason had hit me. The night of homecoming, his tense jaw when I was catcalled. It all made too much sense now.

"No... no, it was an accident." I tried to turn my face away, waiting for him to step back, but he didn't. Instead he leaned even closer, so his bare chest first brushed, and then landed solidly against mine. I stilled, every inch of my body suddenly aware of its particular nerve endings. I felt the way you might when a puppy crawls onto your lap, like one wrong move and you'll scare it away.

Finally, he did move back, and I saw that he had reached over my shoulder to grab a hand towel there. I didn't move while he held it against the blood trickling from my face, even when his thumb accidentally brushed against the skin under my ear.

"It's almost one." I whispered after awhile.

He shrugged again, biting his lip as he adjusted the towel. "I'll just crash here. Not like it would be the first time."

I know.

Silence again, for I don't know how long. Again, I was the one who broke it, which was unusual. Normally he was the one who wouldn't shut up. I don't know if he was drunk, or high, or just tired; honestly I don't know if he was even fully awake, he just wasn't acting like himself. Well, maybe that's not entirely right. He was still Noah, I could see that clearly, just a different side of him, a side I hadn't seen before. Clark Kent, exposed only in the dark.

"Lana and Lexi will be wondering where I am."

He waited another moment before finally pulling the cloth back. It stung a bit as he did so, and I could see the rusty red streaks of dried blood staining it. We'd been sitting there for longer than I'd thought.

"You can stay with me. If you want." He said quietly, and raised the hand that had just set the towel down to tuck my hair behind my ear. "I have my sweatshirt in the other room, you could put it on and take off your bra under it. Alana's bed is more comfortable than that couch in the basement, believe me, and I don't mind sleeping on the floor." His voice was breathy and faster than usual, as if he was...

Shy.

He was being shy, I realized, an emotion I didn't even know he possessed.

I don't know if it was the alcohol, or the time of night, or everything I had just learned about him. It may have been no more than the streak of light from the hallway falling across his chest. Whatever it was, though, we had somehow switched roles. He felt shy, and I... I felt brave.

"I don't want you to sleep on the floor." I whispered before I could talk myself out of it.

He looked up so fast he nearly hit his head against mine. His hand, which was still in my hair, slid down to cup my cheek. He tilted his head to the side, as if questioning. His eyes, like always, caught the nonexistent light in the room. I remember a line from some cheesy John Green book, about people always celebrating the easy attractiveness of blue eyes, but that brown eyes were really uniquely special. I had to admit, he was right. Noah's eyes weren't clear or translucent or watery, they didn't change color, as they would have been if they were blue or green or grey. Instead their consistent inky blackness was comforting, and constant, even if nothing else about him ever was.

"Harmony?" He whispered finally. He didn't try to kiss me, but he didn't move his hand from my face either.

He was leaning into me, I could see the distance between us shrinking until we were breathing the same air. His breath was warm without being humid, and he smelled like smoke. I closed my eyes, and behind them I could see my life. I could see the change that letting him into it would make. I could see myself doing it anyway.

This is the part where he turns to stone.

The voice came out of nowhere, and my eyes opened.

To tell you that I didn't want him would be a lie. To tell you that I had been implying something other than the obvious when those words left my lips would be pointless. Maybe I should be ashamed of what I was thinking, considering the events of the night, considering the events of the past year and a half, but I'm not. I was 15 years old, and while there are so many things I've done in my life that I regret as I sit here writing these words, the things I wanted to do with Noah that night aren't one of them. I don't know much, hardly anything really, but I do know that I loved that kid in the kind of way that people write songs you play at weddings about. No matter what I learned about him, no matter what may have made him irredeemable to anyone else, I loved him. I wish I had more to say for my life, and I'll admit that I'm ashamed that I don't, but it's better than nothing, and I hope I've made it clear to you. And Noah, if you ever have the unfortunate experience of reading this dreadful piece of shit that only the most generous of souls would call my life, then for God's sake, at least know that you were loved.

The only problem was that you didn't love me, did you?

I took a step away from him. I could see my reflection in his eyes; my hair of writhing snakes, my red eyes and putrid green skin. I could see him turning to stone in front of me.

"Harmony?" He said again, this time with some concern.

You have to go cut your head off now.

"Noah, you should sleep in Alana's bed. A-alone. They're probably wondering where I am. I should go." I sidestepped him, my vision blurry.

"What? Harm, no, talk to me." He cut around me so he was between me and the stairs. With his hands on my shoulders, he leaned into me so I had nowhere to look but his eyes.

"Noah. No." I shook my head, but he only shook his back even harder.

"No, Harmony. I'm not a mind reader. I can't listen to the things that you're not saying out loud. Okay? You have to tell me. Please. Just tell me." His voice was breaking.

I don't want you to start something you can't finish.

I don't want you to make a choice that you'll regret.

I don't want to add any more shit to your life.

I don't want to lose you, ever, and the only way I can be sure that I won't is if I make sure I never really have you.

In my head I told him. But the things that we say in our heads never matter as much as the things we don't say out loud.

"You don't tell me everything." I finally managed to say back.

His face fell, and his hold on my shoulders loosened. He opened his mouth as if to respond, but didn't. He knew he had nothing to say. I saw my oppourtunity and ducked under his arm, then down the stairs a few steps.

Why did I run from him? I don't know. I don't have an explanation to give you besides the fact that I was Medusa, and I didn't want to turn him into stone.

I managed to reach the bottom of the stairs before I said anything else, but at the base, I knew I had to say one more thing. Something that would cause me the pain I deserved, and give him the escape from me he needed.

I turned around to see him standing at the top of the stairs, his head in his hands.

"Noah." I said. "I *do* know how I feel about Devante. I like him, and he's who I want to be with."

The only tears on my cheeks were made of blood.

My attitude toward going out and eventually sleeping with Devante can probably be inferred by my not even listing it as one of the major eight events of that year. He was a nice guy, and I enjoyed his company about as much as I enjoyed everything else in my life- not enough. My mom liked him, and he and Rory could talk about football together. He and Stands With a Fist didn't bond, however. He said he was a dog person.

All in all, though, we got along. When we weren't hanging out at my house, I went to his basketball games, although the season was almost over. He was talented, he was trying for a scholarship, leading point guard. He had it in the bag, for the most part, besides one glaring obstacle. Noah Andrade played point guard.

Me and Devante didn't talk about Noah any more than we talked about anyone else, but when we did, it was obvious what his feelings toward him were. They had known each other since they were six, they had grown up together, played sports together- they were practically brothers. Devante loved Noah the same way everyone else did, with a kind of awe and jealousy that would never really go away. When your best friend was always the cutest, most charming, most talented kid in the room, you couldn't help feeling like second best. They weren't in competition- Noah would have put Devante first in anything and everything, but Devante didn't want charity. He wanted to be better, and he wanted his chance to prove it.

February second, a Friday night, was a big game for them. Jacksonville High, a leading recruiter of kids from all over the area, was seated to move to the championship game. Unless, of course, Rosemont could miraculously turn around a three game losing streak and get in their way.

By the end of the third quarter, things weren't looking great. We were down five with 30 seconds on the clock, when number 5, Noah Andrade, got the ball. He dribbled down the court like the other team wasn't even there, dodging and turning around the defensive players as if he knew what they were going to do before they did. My eyes found Devante, watching him. My boyfriend was talented, but it was a once in a million kid who could play like that, and he knew it. Noah, Noah just had something that the rest of the guys didn't.

He got up to the basket when a center for the other team, this 6'4" kid whose number was actually 64, and who looked like he belonged in college, appeared out of nowhere. Noah was half his size, and there was no way he was getting to the basket without literally plowing through the kid. The coach was screaming at him, the crowd was losing it's shit, and this neanderthal was dripping sweat into his face, but Noah wasn't fazed. I could see it in his face- he was getting to that basket, one way or another.

He ducked, spun, and fit his elbow into the kid's stomach. When he straightened up, the center was on his ass on the ground, and he stood at the three point line. He let the ball sail through the air, swishing through the net without even bumping the backboard.

He barely had time to catch his breath before the ref blew his whistle. "Penalty foul! Aggressive playing!"

Noah spun around, sweat flying off his hair. His temper, always dormant just beneath his laid back demeanor, flared. *Oh Christ.*

"What the fuck, ref? He was right on top of me!"

He was livid, and he shoved off the coach when he tried to console him. "That's a bullshit call, and you know it!" The ref had turned and walked away, but Noah pushed him in the back. "I'm fucking talking to you!"

The ref, a balding white guy who looked like he'd had his job a few too many years, was not amused. "One more move like that and you're out of the game kid, you hear me?"

The Jacksonville center smirked and said something that I couldn't hear from the bleachers, but Noah certainly did. He whipped around, his fist flying through the air without hesitation. Mercifully, Devante caught his arm just before it made contact with the kid's nose, though you could see it took all his effort just to hold him back.

"Take a hike, Andrade." Coach Prout, who I'd become relatively familiar with since dating Devante, pushed Noah off the court.

"DON'T FUCKING CALL ME THAT." He lunged again, fuming, but his teammates caught him and hauled him back. He shook them off and stormed off the court as the buzzer went off. One quarter left to play. The penalty held, score was 55 to 60.

I caught up with Devante on the side of the court where he was getting a drink.

"If he's not back here by the time the quarter starts, you're starting, Harris." I arrived just in time to hear Prout say. Devante swallowed, and I touched his arm.

"Hey." I tried to smile.

He returned it, but anyone could tell he was nervous out of his mind. "I can't start." He confessed quietly.

"What do you mean? There are scouts everywhere. This is your shot."

He shook his head, biting his lip. "Noah's better than me. Don't tell me that he's not, you know it's true. If I start and I lose this game for us..." He trailed off.

"If Noah can't control his temper, he doesn't deserve to play." I told him. I knew there was no point in arguing with him about who was better. He wasn't being humble, he was stating a fact that everybody knew. No one was as daring, as fast, as on top of every play as Noah. He worked practice harder than anyone else on the team, he insisted on playing all of every game, he showed up even on the days he missed school. No one wanted it more than he did, but he was going to ruin it for himself.

"Will you find him?" Devante asked me. His eyes were pleading. "There's two minutes before the final quarter. Please, will you make sure he's here?"

I touched his arm. I did care for him. Not as much as I should have, but I truly did. Please believe that. "Okay."

I kissed him briefly, then quickly left the gym.

I knew Noah would be in the locker room, and there was a strict no girls policy, but what did I care? It smelled like old sweat and body odor, but I barely noticed. He was sitting on the bench under one of the only working lights, his head in his hands.

"There's less than two minutes before the final quarter."

He looked up, but didn't start. His eyes were red, and sweat dripped from his nose. "I'm not playing."

Suddenly, I was angry. "Well, that's just great, Noah. Cause you're the only one on the team, right? If you don't play, if you lose this game, it doesn't matter at all, does it? No one else loses a scholarship, no one else gets hurt. It's all about you, isn't it?"

"Fuck you." His voice was choked.

"No, fuck you. You need to pull your head out of your ass and get on the fucking court."

"Goddammit!" He jumped up and slammed his fist into the locker next to my head. I didn't jump. No matter how mad he was, he would never hurt me. I knew that.

"I don't give a shit, Harmony. Okay? I DON'T GIVE A SHIT WHAT HAPPENS." Looking in his eyes, I saw for the first time what I had seen in Cameron's. Something wild, and unhinged.

Something broken.

"I don't believe that." I said quietly. He was trying to scare me, he was trying to get me to leave, but I wasn't going anywhere. Maybe that made me an idiot, but I wanted to be right about him. I wanted him to be who I believed he was.

"Well, you're just stupid, then." He said, but the anger in his voice had changed. It wasn't gone, but it was no longer directed at the world around him. He may not have known it, but he was angry with himself, and I could tell.

I took his hand and brought him back to the bench. He sat down silently and didn't wince while I held the corner of my shirt to his bleeding knuckles.

"If you don't play, we'll lose this game. You're the best one out there, Noah, and you know it. The team needs you to keep your head."

He shook his head. "I can't do it."

"Honestly, Noah, I don't really think there's anything that you can't do. You can't fuck with me, I know you care about that team. They're counting on you. *Devante* is counting on you. This is his shot. If you guys win this game, he's got a chance at a scholarship. You both do." I glanced at the clock. Less than a minute left. His hand was shaking in mine, and the blood flow was still steady. The med kit was on the floor, and I grabbed the gauze to wrap it temporarily.

"Do you love him?" His voice was quiet. I could feel him looking at me, but I didn't look up.

"It doesn't matter."

I don't know what his facial expression was, but the veins in his arm tightened. He was quiet for a moment before he spoke again. "I'm not gonna get a scholarship, Harmony. Not after the shit I just pulled. Teams want my talent, sure, but nobody wants me. They all just wanna use me."

No, Noah. Not everyone.

"Then be more than your talent. Be *more*. Go out there, and, and be Superman."

He smiled slightly. I finished wrapping his hand and stood up. 10 seconds till game time. "What have you got to lose?"

He closed his eyes, and got to his feet. Touching my shoulder, he passed me silently, and went to the door.

"Noah." I called after him. He stopped, but didn't turn around. Five seconds.

I swallowed. "No." I said. "I don't."

He turned around quickly, his hand on the door, and this time I looked at him. I had that feeling, for the third time. That feeling that if he looked at me for another five seconds, he'd feel it too.

But there weren't five seconds left. We only had three.

He left the locker room, and I followed a few moments after. Back in the gym, I made eye contact with Devante, who mouthed "thank you." I nodded, and sat back down. My eyes were on the scoreboard as the buzzer went off.

The fourth quarter was hell. Fouls, penalty shots, dirty playing on both teams. With less than a minute remaining, we were down two, and again Noah had the ball. He dribbled down the court, ducking in between the other kids before they even knew he was there. Up to the three point line, and again, number 64 was bearing down on him. He froze, his face impossible to read, when suddenly he looked up at me.

What are you doing? There was nothing I could say. I didn't know what was going on inside his head, hell if anybody did. Whatever it was, though, he had decided something. Seven seconds on the clock.

Honestly Noah, I don't really think there's anything that you can't do.

"Time out!" He called, straightening up. Murmurs of confusion ran through both the court and the stands.

He set the ball down and jogged over to where Prout was standing. They had a whispered conversation, with the coach shaking his head and Noah nodding rapidly. He gestured to Devante incessantly, and finally, Prout threw up his hands.

Noah nodded at Devante, who looked shocked and terrified. He shook his head, but Noah pushed him onto the court. Devante picked up the ball and got into position, looking back at Noah one last time, as though he hoped he would shake his head and say he had been kidding.

Instead, he nodded, crossing his arms. The ref blew the whistle, and every eye in the room was on Devante.

He faced the center in front of him, and took a deep breath. Then he faked left, lunged right, and spun to the left again at the last second. 64 fell for it, and dove to the right as Devante shot the ball as hard as he could for the hoop. It hit the backboard, spun around the rim, and tipped into the basket, just as the buzzer went off.

The score was 63 to 64. Rosemont was going to the championship.

The crowd went crazy. The whole team rushed past the stunned Jacksonville players onto the court, where they gathered around Devante, literally screaming. The scouts were scribbling madly on their clipboards. Coach Prout was actually crying. But I wasn't paying attention to any of it.

Noah Andrade stood on the side of the court, his arms still crossed, smiling just slightly. He turned to me, and his eyes softened. He wasn't getting recruited, and we both knew it.

I love you, Noah.

I don't know if he knew it, but I know I wasn't imagining it when I saw his eyes brighten.

"Did you see it?" Devante ran over to me and lifted me off the ground. I laughed.

"I told you you could do it."

He grinned and kissed me.

"Are you gonna go out with the team?" I asked him, and he nodded.

"Yeah, I kinda have to. I'll call you later though, okay?" He was trying to sound apologetic, but he couldn't keep the smile off his face. I told him yeah of course, I didn't mind, and that I was proud of him, and kissed him again.

I left the gym after the crowd had diminished. I wanted to run into Noah again, but I didn't, and maybe that was for the best. I don't know what I would have said to him. I walked home alone, past the 7/11 and Freddie's on Main Street. That night, no one bothered me.

Before I went to bed, I pulled out my phone. One message from Devante that I must have missed on the walk home.

Devante: imma be out late but im glad u were there bbg, ill call u tomorrow <3

I replied sweet dreams, then went to turn my phone off, but somehow ended up in Noah's contact instead. I chewed my lip, my fingers hovering over the screen. Finally, I typed out five words.

Im proud of u, Superman.

He replied immediately.

Noah: i did it for u

I read the text 10 times, but I didn't respond.

There was nothing else to say.

So. Anyway. Basketball season ended. Devante had college offers from more than five different schools. Noah had none.

Me and Devante kept hanging out. He was a completely different person now that he was finally getting recognized. Always happy and laughing and wanting to celebrate. He partied almost every weekend, and I tried to keep up as best I could, going out more, to Alana's house and his and sometimes Jaideson's. The whole group was usually there, with one blinding exception. Noah was conspicuously absent, and the fact that no one mentioned it only made it harder to ignore. I saw Jared a couple of times, and wanted to ask him, but I was afraid of the answer. I shouldn't have cared at all, anyway.

The only problem with this new development in my life, besides the obvious, was that most of the parties happened Friday nights, and, having previously had nothing to do, I had told my boss I could work the late shift on weekends. Now that I'd been working there for a couple of months, schedules had been established, and it wasn't like I could just change things around. Devante was upset, he said he didn't mind just hanging out with me at Freddie's while I closed, but I could tell that he would always rather be out with his boys. I told him so, and said that I wasn't offended. Frankly, I would have been more worried if he *had* actually wanted to hang around that place.

Freddie's wasn't so bad once I got used to it. Having money on hand wasn't really something I needed, so even though I was only making minimum wage, pretty soon my finances added up. By April, I had almost $2,000 saved. The money wasn't why I kept working though, just like the sex and company wasn't why I stayed with Devante. I did both so I could be doing something normal, so that maybe I could convince myself that I *was* normal, that I was growing out of a phase. Not that it worked.

April 31st of my Sophomore year was a Saturday night. Devante, Gio, Lexi, Jaideson, and a couple other kids were hanging out, and presumably getting stoned, at Alana's. I was glad to have an excuse not to go- I wasn't built to party every weekend, especially since I didn't smoke, and that was the major pastime. I was probably the only kid in my grade who would have rather worked a four hour closing shift at a shitty diner instead of being out with my boyfriend, but then again, I was probably the only kid in my grade who did a lot of things.

I'm on my way home, I texted my mother at 12:30. It was the last correspondence recorded on my phone that night until I got home around one, and later the police would use it as evidence to try and place me that night.

I left the diner and started on my way home. I was used to the early morning sounds of the city by then, and I wasn't nervous as I walked down the street toward the 7/11. That is, until I heard the police sirens.

They were coming from behind me, back toward the high school, and at first I didn't think anything of them, until the alarm system of the convenience store started blaring. People were shouting inside the store, and the noise of breaking glass and doors slamming echoed up and down the otherwise unusually quiet street.

"Fuck you!" Someone screamed, a man's voice. "Little hard ass punks! Get the fuck outta my store, assholes!" There was a heavy thud, and then an even heavier one. The man's voice stopped.

"Holy shit, man!"

"We gotta move, now."

Someone's fist slammed through the front window of the store, shattering glass into the street. I stepped back off the curb, and watched unseen as the scene unfolded in the dim lighting of the burglar alarm and the street lamp.

Three figures ran through the smashed door, their sneakers crunching on the broken glass that was scattered around the front of the store. They all wore hoodies and it was two dark to see their faces anyway, but I could tell that the first two were significantly taller than the third. The three of them ran right past me, stuffing handfuls of cash and cigarettes and other stolen shit into their pockets as they went. I was confused as to where they were going at first, there was nothing but woods and the dump behind the store. They weren't slowing down as they approached the chain link fence that kept animals off the street, and my confusion was resolved as one by one, they clambered over it and disappeared into the night. The first two made it over okay, but the third, the smallest one, got caught. The sleeve of his hoodie was stuck in a tear in the wire, and he struggled with it, obviously panicking. The sirens were getting closer.

"I'm stuck!" He screamed desperately.

"Come on!" One of the voices yelled, but neither of the other boys came back.

Finally, the third boy tore his arm out of his hoodie, ripping the fabric as he did so. He freed himself of the fence and jumped over it, landing hard on the other side. He was up and running after his friends just as the police cars rounded the corner, leaving the remains of his sweatshirt on the top of the fence.

I could hear the store owner begin to get up inside the store, so I didn't worry myself about checking to see if they'd really hurt him. Instead, as if walking on feet that weren't connected to my brain, I went over to the fence. Three sets of footprints were haphazardly scattered in the dirt, but other than that, there was no trace of any boys. Besides, of course, the sweatshirt.

I freed it from the top of the fence, turning around quickly to see if the police had arrived yet. They were coming up the street, but were still a ways off. I shook the dirty sweatshirt out, and held it up to the light coming from the streetlamp. The flashing lights of the burglar alarm illuminated gray fabric.

And the Lakers logo in the middle of it.

I stared at the piece of clothing in my hands.

My throat felt like sandpaper, and my heart may have actually stopped beating. Only one word registered in my mind.

Noah.

Behind me, I heard the first cop car screech to a halt in front of the store. The noise from the sirens was deafening. Turning around, I saw the officer jump out of his car and run into the store. I saw two more patrol cars peel into the parking lot behind it. I saw the lights, I heard the yelling and cursing, I smelt the gas dripping from the pumps in front of the store. I saw, I heard, I smelt. I felt.

I hesitated for a fraction of a second, then I stuffed Noah's hoodie under my jacket, and ran home.

– PART NINE –

Liability

You gotta be careful who you mess with around here. You never know what some kids might do.

I let myself in the back door around one. Rory's keys were on the counter again, along with his jacket and baseball cap. When I left the kitchen, only the jacket and hat remained.

If I were you, I wouldn't mess with him.

The police sirens still stalked the streets of my neighborhood, but inside my bedroom, everything was drowned out by the voices in my head.

McCane told him he bet he had, and that he was just like his father.

Just like his father. Just like his brothers. Three boys running out of the store, the first two bigger than the third. Three sets of footprints in the dirt, the smallest trailing after the bigger two.

Was I like my father? A man I hadn't seen since I was in diapers? Would I recognize him if I saw him now? Would he recognize me? Would Hannah's father, the man who raised me, recognize me, if he was still alive?

Certain things, well, certain things set everybody off, right?

Yes, certain things set everybody off. I rolled up my sleeve, exposing the winter pale skin of my arm. Thin lines like lace, drawn in purple and pink racing their way across my skin. Like a Valentine's card. Devante had given me a card like that on Valentine's Day.

I looked at the scars on my arm. So much pain, so much desperation, and all it amounted to was a few pathetic lines on my wrist. Most of them were starting to fade, and soon I would have nothing to show for it at all. Not this time, though. This time I'd make them stay.

No. 'he's not' either.

I drew the first line against my skin. Hard, but not hard enough.

Fuck off, Harmony. Now.

My teeth gritted involuntarily as I yanked the blade roughly across my skin. Blood spurted from the cut, staining my sheets, but I could barely feel it. I needed to feel it.

Hey Harm. Idk what got into Noah he can be such a dick. Hope u ok.

Fuck off, Harmony. Hope you okay, Harmony. Who was Harmony? Who the fuck was she?

Are you still mad at me?

No, Noah. I'm not mad at you. I never was.

Not so brave now, are you?

Not so brave now. What was it my mother had said? If I was trying to be brave or sexy or whatever, it wasn't working. All I was was ugly. It was all I had ever been. I pressed the blade harder against my wrist, digging it to the bone despite the blinding pain. Ugly. Stupid. Pathetic. Harmony.

There's a lot that you don't know about my brother.

I wished I could tell Jared that I'd finally figured it out. I would never know anything about Noah. How could I, when I didn't know anything about myself? There wasn't anything to know. I was nothing. It was all nothing.

Sometimes kids act like they don't even got mamas.

Okay. Enough. Please stop. You won. I get it. Stop now. I can't do it anymore. Please, just stop.

I was looking for you. Alana said it would be okay if we went upstairs…

Please. No more. Stop. I couldn't even see my arm, there was so much blood.

One more move like that and you're out of the game kid, you hear me?

Stop. Just stop.

If Noah can't control his temper, he doesn't deserve to play.

Please.

*I don't give a shit, Harmony. Okay? I DON'T GIVE A SHIT WHAT
HAPPENS.*

Stop.

But it didn't.

It never would.

One more step.

And then a million more.

"Harmony, do you ever think about taking your own life?"
Of course I did. It wasn't going anywhere on it's own.

May second was a Monday. I showed up to school on time, or rather,
what was left of me did. Noah Andrade did not.

The third was a Tuesday. Again, I was there. Again, Noah wasn't.

His signature grin and sweatshirt were absent from the hallways.
They were absent from the gym, and from the parking lot, and from
the basketball court after school. The grin I could not account for. The
sweatshirt, on the other hand, was in my backpack.

Finally, Wednesday arrived, and with it, the youngest Andrade brother.
People were talking non stop about the events of the weekend, much of it
had appeared on Live Pd. Three teenage boys, approximated ages between
15 and 20, entered the 7/11 on Main Street at 12:36. After harassing the
clerk and trashing the store, one of them pulled out a knife, and threatened
the cashier. Terrified, he emptied the contents of the register into the boys'
hands, and they made off with it, along with cigarettes, nips, condoms,
and candy bars. Not before one of them, however, landed the store owner
a heavy blow to his head. Three stitches.

No suspects had been named, and the police had no leads. Cameron
had been right. The security cameras didn't work. That left the police with
nothing to go on. No evidence whatsoever.

Because my bag was heavy with it.

I didn't know what I was going to do with the sweatshirt at all until I saw him. I wanted to give it to him, to keep it, to throw it away, to burn it. I wanted to want to give it to the police. I wanted it to be over.

Then I saw him Wednesday morning, and I made up my mind. It had never really been a choice anyway.

"Noah?"

He was standing at the bubbler after second period, with Andy and Jason. There were only five minutes between each class, so I knew I didn't have any to waste.

"Hey, million dollar baby." He turned around, smiling. "Do you want a hug?"

He didn't give me time to answer before stepping forward to envelop me in his arms. I let my eyes fall closed for just a moment. Just one moment to breathe him in. One moment to pretend that everything was okay.

He was wearing a black sweatshirt with the American flag on the front. I pulled away.

"You okay?" He looked concerned, and I bit my lip against the truth.

"Yeah. We need to talk though. Now."

He nodded. One thing about Noah, you never had to explain yourself. He just knew.

"Sure. Guys, I'll catch you later." He slapped palms with both boys and they nodded, before walking off. The hallway was still busy enough, full of couples and friends and boys shouting to each other from 20 feet away.

"What's up?" He turned to me with a grin. I took a deep breath, and looked him in the eye.

Then I pulled his hoodie out of my bag.

"Lose something?"

I don't think I can describe in accurate detail just how quickly his face fell. I had never seen eyes so big, or lips so frozen, or skin so pale. For the first time in possibly his entire life, Noah Andrade was speechless.

"Look, I'm gonna say something right now, and you're gonna listen. Okay?" He blinked, and closed his mouth before nodding.

"Whatever it is that's going on, whatever you been doing, you are better than this shit, Noah. I don't know if that's all you need- for someone to say that out loud to you, but if it is then I'm saying it. Don't be who people think you are. Okay? You are better than this. You- you're everything, Noah."

It was out of my mouth before I'd even know it was in my head. I'd planned to just walk up to him, give him the sweatshirt, and leave. Once I looked in his eyes though, that plan was out the window.

I thrust the hoodie, washed and mended, into his arms, then took a step back. The bell rang, and the few remaining stragglers in the halls hurried to class.

"We're friends, okay?" I told him. His eyes were so full they looked like the were leaking out of their sockets, and his knuckles were white around the sweatshirt. "That means I got your back. No matter what."

That's enough, Harmony. That's enough now.

Okay.

I turned on my heel and walked to class, leaving him standing by the water fountain.

I didn't look back.

Enough was enough.

PART TEN

Waiting for Superman

After that, things started to happen very fast. In asking around, the police acquired the employee records of three of the businesses neighboring the 7/11 on Main Street. Ruby's Hair and Nails, Tai on the Go Takeout, and Freddie's All Night Diner. No one had clocked out of Tai on the Go before two, and Ruby's closed at 10. That meant that, theoretically speaking, I was the only person who had been in a 50 foot radius of the scene of the crime within 20 minutes of it occurring, and that was good enough for the cops.

They called me down to guidance for the first time on May sixth, but I didn't budge. I wasn't there, I didn't see anything, hear anything, or know anything at all. Cameron and Joel Andrade had police records and hadn't been heard from in over a week? It was all news to me. Jared Andrade could provide an alibi for the night in question, but the fourth brother, the youngest, could not. Wasn't there any chance, any chance at all that I had seen Noah Andrade on Main Street that night?

No. There was not.

A promise was a promise, and Freshman year Noah had promised me that he would have my back no matter what. He hadn't broken his, so I wasn't going back on mine. I don't know if he remembered what I had told him the night of Homecoming, that telling someone you were in their corner was another way of saying I love you, but I did.

Not that it mattered. None of it mattered at all.

I was winding down. I could feel my body beginning to fail to function as my mind deteriorated. Nothing made it better anymore. There wasn't an antidote to my problem, not even a temporary one, because I *was* the problem. I didn't even have the energy to fake it anymore. No more smiling, no more friends, no more homework, no more boyfriend. I broke it off with Devante less than a week into May, and honestly I couldn't even tell you the excuse I gave him. In all his bipolarness, Noah, the one who had told me not to go out with him in the first place, confronted me about it at lunch.

"I can't believe you left him." He said. "Do you know how bad this is gonna fuck him up?"

I didn't respond, just let him yell. It was the only time we had spoken in weeks. After the day I returned his sweatshirt, he had acted as if I didn't exist, and I followed suit. I knew that his acting like a dick about Devante was just him venting the stress he was feeling, and that it was my fault for tying myself to that stress. I *knew* that, but it didn't change the fact that I had lost him, and in doing so, I had lost the last pillar holding me up.

I kept thinking back to that day, the day I called Jacob Santanuno's phone and received nothing but the dial tone. I kept thinking about the moment I put the phone back on the receiver and stared at it, waiting for it to ring, waiting for someone to call me and tell me that my whole life so far had been a dream, and it wouldn't be much longer before I woke up and it all went away. I kept waiting for it to stop. And then it didn't.

Every minute felt like that moment.

Alcohol didn't make it better, but I told myself that it did. I had lost any appetite or interest in food I may have once had. It was becoming pretty clear that one way or another, I wasn't gonna be around for much longer. I spent longer and longer just summing up the will to get out of bed every morning, to shower, get dressed, and complete any other basic task. My mother couldn't have been as oblivious as she seemed, but I think I've already made it clear that she was pretty done with me. She scheduled more appointments with Dr. James, but even that was futile. My mother was done with me, my therapist was, my boyfriend was, my friends were, and Noah was. We were all done.

Monday. May 10th. One week ago. That's how far we've come. In the past 70 pages of this pathetic piece of shit that sums up my life, we've come almost two whole years. And now it's over. This is it. Finally, finally we can stop.

Well, almost.

Because my story wouldn't be complete if I left out the events of the past seven days. They didn't shape me in any particular way, or affect my outcome one way or another. That's not why I have to tell you. No, the reason why is Noah. Because if anyone ever finds this and picks it up and manages to read the entire thing without drinking a gallon of bleach, I want them to know this. I want them to know that no matter what else, no matter what people will say about him, he was a boy who did one thing right. I need you to know that. I owe him that much.

Monday started just like any other day. I stared at my ceiling for 15 minutes before dragging myself out of bed and monotonously completing the steps needed to get out the door. School dragged by, each hour fading into the next with the merciless drone of the wall clocks. Three periods. I made it through three periods before receiving my daily dose of self loathing.

I was walking to class, Intro to Economics, past the bubbler where I'd had my last real conversation with Noah a few weeks before, when I walked right into someone.

In a state of deja vu, I looked up to see a familiar face staring down at me. Sure enough, it was Jason. He was supposed to have graduated the year before, but with his GPA, he hadn't even come close to making the cut. I hadn't really given him any thought since the day of the fight, when he'd been arrested. To be honest, I hadn't even realized that he was back in school. No, wait. That's not true. I had seen him once since. I couldn't remember when.

"Watch where the fuck you're going." He said gruffly, stepping back quickly so I just about fell over. He laughed, and his friends did too.

Two years before, I would have given it right back to him. Thrown my bag to the ground, made a scene, raised my voice, demanded an apology.

I thought the girl I was two years ago was in bad shape. I wonder if she would even recognize the girl I am right now.

The girl I was a week ago just stumbled forward until I regained my feet. I put my hand on the wall to steady myself and took a deep breath. Then I went to keep walking.

"Bitch I'm talking to you."

Don't walk away from me, bitch.

I stopped. I could feel him as he got closer to me, till finally his hand landed on my waist. His breath was in my ear when he whispered, "You're supposed to apologize when you walk into someone."

Sorry. Just say sorry, Harmony, and go to class.

I closed my eyes and willed myself to say it, but the words wouldn't come. I wasn't sorry. I wasn't anything at all.

He pushed me up against the wall, roughly, and again I stumbled. This time he caught me, and shoved my shoulder into the side of the water fountain. The water fountain. That's where I had seen him before. He had been standing next to it two Wednesday's ago, talking to-

"Then again, maybe if you let me do what I want, we can forget about the whole thing." He was leaning in so close to me that no one else could have heard him, although a lot of people were watching. So many pairs of eyes, none of them making contact with mine. So many mouths, and not one of them opened. How many teachers were there in that building? How hard would it have been for one of those kids, *just one kid,* to run and get one? How hard?

I don't know I don't know I don't know.

Jason's hand, sweaty and greedy, slid up the front of my shirt. His back and the water fountain blocked me from the camera, but I doubt he cared one way or another. Jason, Cameron, the boys in the car the night of homecoming. They were all the same. I was nothing to all of them. It was all I ever was.

He gripped my side to an extent that should have been painful, and leaned down toward the collar of my shirt. I knew if I just shut my eyes and thought about something else, it would be over before I knew it. The bell had to ring sooner or later. His hand snaked higher and higher, past my stomach, up to my ribs. His fingertips touched the edge of my bra. In a second they would be under it.

Except that a second passed, and they weren't.

They weren't because out of nowhere, someone broke free of the crowd and grabbed Jason. He was so caught off guard that the kid, despite being half his size, was able to throw him off of me instantly with almost superhuman force. Then again, people had always said Noah Andrade could do crazy things when he was angry.

"What the fuck?" Jason slammed against a locker. He staggered, straightening up while he nursed a bloody nose. He stared at his hand in shock. "You broke my nose, you little shit!"

Panting, Noah rushed forward and slammed into him again. The two of them fell to the floor, and kids scattered out of the way. Jason was bigger by at least a hundred pounds, but Noah had the upper hand. I had never seen anything like it, and I thought I had seen him mad before. But never, and I mean *never* like this.

He grabbed Jason by the hair and slammed his head into the floor, then yanked him up again by the shirt. He held him while he landed two good blows to the side of his face, one after the other.

"DON'T EVER FUCKING TOUCH HER AGAIN, DO YOU HEAR ME?" His fist slammed into Jason's jaw, and came away bloody. "PUT YOUR HANDS ON HER AGAIN AND I WILL FUCKING KILL YOU, YOU CHEAP PIECE OF SHIT. STAY. AWAY. FROM. HER."

Jason pulled an arm free and knocked Noah on the side of the head, hard. He went flying into the lockers across the hall from me. Somewhere, a girl screamed, and for an irrational moment I thought he was dead.

Then he scrambled to his feet. They both did. Noah charged at the bigger boy similarly to the way I had tried to Freshman year, aiming low, for his stomach. He knocked the wind out of him, and the two of them banged into the wall. And that, finally, is when a teacher showed up.

"Noah Andrade!" Mr. Waiter, the gym teacher and my friend, ran into the middle of the circle that had formed with speed impressive for his age. He caught Noah around the waist and yanked him off of Jason firmly, though I could tell that he was surprised by the strength it required.

"What in God's name is going on?" The school resource officer, Mr. Duarte, joined the scene in time to catch Jason's arm before he could land another one to Noah's jaw. The two teachers pulled the boys, both shaking and heaving, away from each other while at least 20 cell phones recorded the whole thing. Both kids were pretty beat up, but there was no question who had won the fight. Jason was sporting a bloody nose, two already blackening eyes, and a handful of teeth falling from the waterfall of blood in his mouth.

"Go the fuck to class before I get you all suspended!" Mr. Waiter bellowed. The group of kids scattered instantly, talking nonstop, but I wasn't sure what to do. I was still trying to process the whole thing.

"Harmony?" Mr. Waiter's voice broke into my thoughts. "Was there anything you wanted to say?"

I looked at Noah. His head was hanging to his chest, but he looked up as if he had felt my eyes on him. I stared at him, trying to gauge anything at all, but his expression was more opaque than ever. A boy with black eyes who gave black eyes. For me. Because he had my back.

"Noah..." I trailed off. I couldn't just leave him. Where had the teachers been when Jason had his hand up my shirt two minutes before? Why did they only show up now, just in time to make the whole thing look like Noah's fault?

"Harmony. Just go." His voice was tense.

"Harmony?" Mr. Waiter said again, and I remembered that there were other people present. "Were you involved in what happened here?" I turned my attention to him. I liked Mr. Waiter a lot. He was patient, and more importantly, he was always fair. Looking in his eyes, I could tell that he knew exactly what had happened, and that at least offered me some relief.

"No." I said slowly. I picked up Noah's bag and my own. Carefully, I picked my way around Duarte and Jason until I could look Noah in the eye. "Here." I handed him his backpack, and it seemed he purposefully brushed his hand against mine when he took the strap. With flushed cheeks, heavy breathing, and eyes brighter than ever, he was a whole different kind of beautiful after the fight.

I turned to go to class, but his hand caught my wrist.

"Harmony." He said softly. "You got my back, I got yours. Okay?" I looked at his hand on my wrist, and remembered the first time it had been there. Over a year ago, in gym class. What had he said that day?

Sometimes, I look at myself and I feel like I see only what everybody else sees, and that's all I've seen for so long that I've forgotten what I really look like.

I looked in his eyes, and remembered all the times they had made me feel safe.

Who was he? A boy who threw snowballs and walked me home and always had my back when I least expected it? Or was he who everyone else said he was- a kid who started fights, who could never control his temper, who was walking down the same road as his father and his brothers?

Both, I realized when I looked at him. Both boys were looking back at me. Superman, and Clark Kent. Noah, and Andrade. He was both. And I loved him.

"Noah." Mr. Waiter said, gently but firmly. He put his hand on his shoulder, and steered him away. It was the last time I ever saw him.

– PART ELEVEN –

Falling Awake

All everyone could talk about was the fight. Both boys had been suspended for the rest of the week, which was fair, probably, though Jason deserved way more, just for the amount of shit he pulled on a daily basis and got away with. The talk amongst the teachers was, I heard, that the superintendent had wanted to suspend Noah for a month, since he technically started the whole thing. It was Mr. Waiter, however, who insisted that you couldn't place blame in a fight like that. He had not, to my knowledge, mentioned to anyone that I had been there at all, for which I was unbelievably grateful. Everyone had seemed to have forgotten about the events leading up to the fight, the events involving me. All anyone cared about was that Noah Andrade had beat the shit out of the toughest kid in school. His friend, at that.

The downside of the whole incident ended up being that people had Noah's name in their mouths again, and word always get around. Kids didn't even have the decency to shut up when a teacher walked into the room. To the police, of course, the fight was a breakthrough. Finally, they had an excuse to go after Noah directly. He was a trouble making kid, a delinquent, currently on in house suspension. Similar events popped up in the pasts of at least two of his older brothers. How could anyone reasonably argue that he *hadn't* been the third perpetrator at the 7/11 that night in April? Only one thing was missing. Proof.

That was where I came in. This morning, the 17th, a week after the fight, I was called down to guidance for the second time. I could tell Mrs. Couto wasn't happy to see me. She hadn't been impressed with my story the first time I'd told it, and she was even less amused when it didn't change. There was nothing that I could have done any better, but I still felt like a liability. Even the possibility of me having witnessed anything was dangerous to Noah, especially because I had a feeling the police knew I was lying.

"I'm asking you again, Harmony. Do you have any idea where Noah was that night?"

I looked up. She was the guidance counselor. The fucking *guidance* counselor.

*Do **you** have any idea, Mrs. Couto? Do you have any idea half the shit that goes on in this school? In this whole fucking town? Do you know that half the kids turn up to class high, and 80% of the time, it's cuz they were smoking in the bathroom? Do you know that none of the teachers care? Do you know that Jason was feeling me up in the middle of the hall the other day, and no one even raised an eyebrow? You're so sure that Noah was vandalizing property, but do you have any idea why? Do you have any idea that it might be because this school system ran over his brothers, and now it's running over him, because it never gave him a chance to be anything other than what it thought he was? Do you have any idea that your job description may concern you more with the fact that a 15 year old girl is sitting in front of you with FAT SLUT carved into her wrist, than with whether she may or may not have witnessed a crime that didn't even happen on school grounds? Tell me, Mrs. Couto, if you could be so courteous, what's your idea about that?*

And then I realized. She didn't care. She knew. She knew all of it, and she didn't give half a shit. That's just not how people work. People don't work like that. They don't care about the things that are important, because so often it's the important things that are the hardest to care about. And I was no different.

She raised an eyebrow. She was waiting for a response, I realized. She was trying to catch me in my lie, to get me to trip up, to say the wrong thing. But I wouldn't. And I wouldn't give her the chance to try again.

"I'm sorry." I said evenly. My voice didn't crack. My hands didn't shake. I met her eyes calmly and defiantly. "I don't."

I was done. I was just so fucking done with all of it.

I left her office without saying goodbye. Jason happened to be walking by as I did so, because of course he was. We made eye contact, and I took in his still swollen and purple face. It had been a week, and both boys were off suspension, but Jason was the only one who was back in school.

He glared, and looked as if he wanted to say something threatening, but thought better of it. I should have been scared- one ass kicking wasn't enough to curb a kid as stupid as Jason forever, he would get his revenge eventually. But I wasn't scared. I knew I wouldn't give him the chance to try again, either.

I went back to class, but didn't absorb anything. Jess sat with me at lunch and tried to engage me in conversation, but I wasn't having it. I told her I was tired, not caring that it was the same excuse I'd given for the past few months. It didn't seem like she cared either, to be honest. Like I said. We were all done.

Nothing felt different when the last bell rang. No one said anything memorable. The hallways didn't feel longer or shorter. The bus ride home wasn't quiet or somber. The world wasn't saying goodbye to me just because I was leaving it. That's just not how it works, I've realized.

I got home and fed the cat. That stupid, pathetic cat. Stands With a Fist, what a dumb name for such a lazy, privileged animal. The cat that had hissed at Noah until he started to pet it. The cat that had dropped a dead mouse outside my door the morning after the fight. It had followed me to the bus stop that morning, too. The cat that Rory always came back for. Stupid. I hated that fucking cat.

He hissed at me indignantly, as though sensing my mood. Whether cats can actually do that, though, I don't know.

"What the fuck do you want, huh?" I said, too loudly. He should have been spooked, but instead he just stared at me, tail twitching. "WHAT?" I said again. I stepped closer to him. Still, he just stared. Stupid, fucking cat.

I picked him up. He was old, fat, and heavy. Like limp fur in my arms. He didn't struggle, or hiss, or anything. I rubbed my face against the rough fur of his scruff. "What?" I said again, softer this time. He still didn't respond. I held him tighter. I wanted to cry, but I couldn't. Stupid. It was all so stupid.

The cat became too heavy, eventually, and time was ticking away, so I had to put him down. My shirt was covered in fur.

"See what you did?" I asked him, gesturing to the fabric. He just sat there, licking his whiskers. Whatever.

The stairs, next. 15 of them. 15 steps. One million steps. Just one more, though, right?

Just one more.

You won't do it. You don't have the guts.

Oh, fuck you. Jokes on you, anyway. This isn't what takes guts, bitch. This isn't what makes you strong. Strong is living. Fighting. This, this is quitting. And I don't care.

It's been nearly 16 years, and this is what it's all added up to. A girl standing in the middle of her bedroom, looking at her reflection, and seeing nothing. That's what I am. Just, nothing.

Noah. Noah was something. He was.... Well, besides everything? He wasn't much. To me at least. I didn't know who I was without him, and because I had never had him, I had never known. I never would. And it was my fault. It was all my fault. There's no blame here. No 13 reasons or some shit like that. Don't you get it? There are no reasons at all.

There's just a woman with salt and pepper hair, and a man who likes movies. There's just a girl who learns a new talent every month, and two fathers who will never be dads, and one dad who can no longer be a father, and three brothers whose names are more famous than they'll ever be. There's just a boy with five scholarship offers to play basketball, and a girl with shiny black hair who never stops smiling. There's just an entitled cat with a culturally appropriated name. There's just a boy with black eyes, and a girl with no reflection. That's all there is. That's all there's ever been. Besides the roof, of course.

I dug my phone out of my pocket and placed it carefully on my bed. Couldn't have any distractions this time. One piece of notebook paper left on my desk, next. Four words.

I love you, Momma.

Just in case she didn't already know.

I opened my window and put one foot on the sill. My legs didn't shake, and that was good. If I fell now, all I'd do was paralyze myself.

Hands on the roof. I barely have the strength to pull myself up anymore, but I managed. Flat on my stomach, then onto my feet. The wind pushed against my frail form, but I held myself still. Not yet.

Harmony.

Harmony.

It's a noun, you know.

I know. I've looked it up over 100 times.

The combination of simultaneously sounded musical notes to produce chords and chord progressions having a pleasing effect.

Pretty. Broken. Pretty, broken girl.

Okay.

Okay.

Okay.

Okay.

The toes of my sneakers peak over the edge of the roof. I look down, but there's nothing on the sidewalk below me. No body this time. Not yet.

I look up, up the street, towards where I know the 7/11 is, although I can't see it. Cars drive by on the street below me, but none of the drivers look up. Why would they?

I wish Noah had been in school. I wish, I wish my mom would come home early. I wish I hadn't stopped talking to Hannah. I wish she had never moved away in the first place. I wish I could erase the last two years of my life. I wish someone had told me when I was little that books are just books, they're not supposed to be real life.

I wish and I wish and I wish.

But wishing doesn't change anything.

That's just not...

That's just not how this works. Fuck.

I'll never know how this works.

One more step, Harmony.

One more step, and then no more. Not a million more. Just one. I think I can manage one.

I lean forward, and then realize I don't know what to do with my eyes. I don't want to look at the ground. I don't want to close them, and be in the dark, because I don't want to be scared. I don't think I could stand being in the dark.

Finally, I just look straight ahead. There's a leaf falling off the branch in front of me, but that doesn't make any sense, because it's summer. Then again, when does anything make sense?

None of this is real, after all.

None of this is real.

I take a breath, tilt my head, clench my fists, watch the leaf, and step off.

In perfect harmony.

PART TWELVE

The Reason

That's the end of Harmony's story. But it's not the end of mine.

My story ends about 15 minutes later, when I got out my backpack to find my phone, and instead my fingers touched a piece of notebook paper. I pulled it out, curious, because let's be honest, it's not like it was a homework assignment or anything. It wasn't written in my handwriting, or in anyone else's that I recognized, but I knew right away that it had to have been her. It took me a minute to figure out when she had been near my bag, but then I remembered. A week before, when she picked it up and handed it to me. I hadn't noticed her put something in it, but she must have.

I read the note maybe five times before it occurred to me to text her. She didn't respond, which shouldn't have scared me, but it did. I had a bad feeling. A really bad feeling. So bad that I told my mom I was going out, and started over to her house. I began walking, but after a minute I started to run. The feeling was getting worse. I had never felt anything like it.

When I got to her street, the police were already there. I got as close as I could, but they wouldn't let me see her.

"Jesus Christ." I heard someone say from the crowd that had gathered behind me. I leaned around the officer in front of me, and then I did see her. Just for a second. Her eyes were open.

It's been 10 years, but still not a day goes by that I don't think about her, and that moment. Not a day goes by that I don't remember sneaking past the cops to get into her house. The door was unlocked, and I went into the kitchen to see the cat sitting in the middle of the floor. He walked up to me and rubbed around my ankles, and I bent down to pet him again. I don't know if she had fed him, but he looked hungry, so I found the cat food and put another scoop in his bowl. Then I went up the stairs to her room. I'd never been in her house, but finding my way around was easy enough. Her bedroom was just as I'd pictured it would be- undisturbed, not particularly clean or messy. The breeze from the open window ruffled the posters on her walls, and the pages of a few books on her desk. I picked a couple of them up and turned the titles over in my mouth- *Meet Kit*, and *The Handmaid's Tale*. I knew her mom would probably be there soon, so I had to clear out. Before I left, though, one last thing caught my eye. A folder full of papers. Computer printouts. At least 70 of them, all neatly typed. It kind of looked like a book, or part of one at least. The first page started with a definition.

I don't know if it was the right thing to do, but I took the folder with me. I still have it. 10 years later, and only now have I decided what I'm going to do with it. 10 years.

10 years, and I still wonder if I could have saved her life with just three words.

It's been 10 years, and I still think about her everyday. I still think about that note she left me, a note that I found less than an hour too late. Just half a page, written in careful, even script.

Noah-

From the Hebrew name נֹחַ (Noach) meaning "rest, repose", derived from the root נוח (nuach). According to the Old Testament, Noah was the builder of the Ark that allowed him, his family, and animals of each species to survive the Great Flood. After the flood he received the sign of the rainbow as a covenant from God.

Our names relate to us. In one way or another. At least, that's what I've heard. It's bullshit, for the most part, probably. For me it is, at least. Harmony doesn't relate to me at all. But you, you're different.

Screw Andrade. Noah is who you are. You're the guy who makes sure everyone gets on the boat. You save people. Ok? That's who you are. That's what I see, when I look at you. I see Superman. I see you, Noah. I always have. Make other people see you, too.

10 years later, and I wonder what she would see if she were to look at me now. Looking in the mirror, right now, do I see what she would want me to?

He's 26, the kid standing in front of me. Not a kid anymore, I guess. Same high fade he had in high school, but shorter now. Peach fuzz finally grew in, too. The scar on his cheek is still there, but tattoos cover the ones on his side now. The Superman symbol over one, and an ark over the other. That's the only ink he has, besides the crudely done cross that's finally starting to fade. There's a ring on his left hand now, too, and pictures of three little kids in his wallet. Two are his, the girls, and one is his nephew, Jared's little boy, Dion. He's almost four, now, and the girls will be two in February. Just a month after his anniversary.

He traded in his sweatshirt for a jersey three years ago, but the colors and the team haven't changed. Purple and yellow, number five. With Lakers printed across the front, and Andrade written on the back. Starting point guard.

That's the man I see when I look in the mirror. And for the first time in 26 years, I can finally look him in the eye.